A WEREWOLF, A VAMPIRE, AND A FAE GO HOME

THE LAST WITCH, BOOK 3

KARPOV KINRADE

EVAN GAUSTAD

http://KarpovKinrade.com

~ ~ ~ ~ ~

Published by Daring Books

~ ~ ~ ~ ~

First Edition
ISBN: 978-1-939559-72-2

~ ~ ~ ~ ~

Book License Notes

Disclaimer

CHAPTER ONE

W *hy?*

WHAT ARE YOU DOING?

Please, talk to me.

Darius stares back at me through narrow eyes. His expression is cold; his face unreadable.

Every effort I make to connect with him, to hear his thoughts and reveal mine, is met with stone-cold silence. I feel his emotions coloring my own, dancing around the edges of my heart, but that's all. Just a steady sense of anger--nothing more, nothing less.

After so many hours of living with souls intertwined, this distance between us feels immeasurable. I can't understand what's changed. My eyes bore into his, trying to find a window into our bond, but I'm shut out.

There's a throbbing pain in my veins. I started to notice it in the passage in the Grand Hall, but ignored it because there was too much going on. Now it's all I can think about, and being near Darius is only making it worse.

Every fiber of my being wants to break down, to scream and cry and fire bolts of lightning into the air, but I push back. It's not that I don't want to show myself to Darius, because I'm sure he can already feel my emotional assault; I don't want to give the satisfaction to Timót. AJ's lying still on the ground, Darius has betrayed my baby, and I'm surrounded by a thunder of dragons, but I will not let my father assume he's taken an ounce of my power.

I keep my eyes on Darius as he walks toward Timót, the vampire's gaze never leaving mine. I'm still baffled by this mental wall he's erected between us. We did a magical blood ritual that was supposed to meld our brains together, and suddenly it's like he's opted out of the contract. And it's not like he's been drifting away--our minds were one and the same less than an hour ago.

Darius arrives next to my father, and the sight of

the two of them side by side makes me clutch my wand so hard I'm worried it will break. Good thing we went with the dragon scale model.

"You didn't have any trouble using the pendant?" my evil father asks my potentially evil blood-bound lover.

Darius nods slowly, his dark, unreadable eyes still on me. His gaze is unsettling, unbreaking and completely lacking expression. If he knows how badly he's wronged me, why won't he look away? If he has some sort of explanation, why doesn't he offer it?

He holds up the *Érintett* medallion that I found in the dragon cave, the one Erzsébet had taken. "I didn't know such a small piece could serve as a portal between realms."

"I spent many years charming that pendant," my father says with a sense of pride, taking the medallion back and putting it around his neck. "I failed repeatedly until an ancient sorcerer gave me the enchanted blood of a Sylph, and now I have the ability to travel at will."

I'm appalled by the coordination between Darius and Timót, and confused by the importance of this pendant I found on a charred corpse in a cave. "Why leave it behind then?"

Timót smiles, a pompous look on his deceitful

face. "Oh, I didn't leave it behind. As it happens, I was there when you came for your scale. After killing the dragon I created the illusion of my death, lying in wait to bring you and your baby here. I can't tell you how disappointing it was that you didn't bring your child. Irresponsible, really."

Thank God I can transfer power into this wand without destroying it, because the rage inside me right now is off the charts. "Thank you so much for the parenting tips. You've always been so good at it."

I'm not going to crack. He's not going to kill me or my baby--not yet, anyway--so I'll keep my cool and hope it ruffles his feathers. He doesn't look like he's enjoying my barbs, but I haven't quite gotten under his skin yet.

"Fortunately," he says, looking at Darius, "the delayed timeline worked in my favor. Now we have an escort to the temple."

Darius doesn't return the look, his gaze still penetrating my own. My ears fill with deafening silence as I try to pry open his thoughts and find out what's happening.

"You'll be happy to know," Timót says to me, "that my dragons and I are going to destroy the sacrificial chambers meant to bleed the Last Witch.

Without that element of the prophecy, the vampires will assume their fate is as good as sealed."

"And then what?" I ask, while keeping my eyes on Darius, as the question readily applies to either traitor.

"Then I'll keep the child while slowly convincing you of the promising life that could be yours. It's hard for you to understand now--"

"Yeah, you've mentioned that," I say, cutting him off. "That's the type of argument someone without a convincing argument says over and over. You're a trash ball and everyone knows it, so let's stop pretending someday I'll understand otherwise and we'll be one big happy family of psychopaths."

My dad flares his nostrils as he takes a deep breath, making a face similar to one I've seen all too many times in the mirror. When he exhales, he's no less angry. "If you weren't such a foolish young girl, maybe you could be made to see the grander themes at play, as your vampire friend managed to do."

"Yeah, well..." The staring match between myself and Darius continues, and it's harder than ever to keep my cool. "He might be garbage, too."

For the first time since he arrived, I feel a blip inside me, a small bubble in our emotional union.

Nothing registers on the vampire's face, but I can sense a tiny wound from my words.

Why? I say again, practically screaming inside my head while trying to keep my face still, hoping that little word will slip through the small crack that's appeared in the wall between us.

Nothing. Trying to connect with him only makes the throbbing in my veins worse.

This tiny sliver of an opening is gone, sealed up tight once again.

I raise my wand, not aiming at Timót, but Darius. I don't know what spell I plan on shouting, I only know I'm at the end of my rope and I either need to find out why he's done this or make him hurt. Since I'm not sure he can feel the pain coursing through me, I might need to see it on his face.

"I'd be careful, Bernadette," Timót says in a disgustingly condescending tone. "I believe Darius is the only vampire who doesn't want you to die. Any harm you cause him won't help you or your child in any way."

My current despair makes it hard to care about what might happen and when. Whatever his intentions, Darius betrayed me. Perhaps he couldn't bear the thought of us being apart, but this wasn't his decision to make, and it wasn't the right choice. I mean, does he think we'll ride off into the sunset together after my daughter's ripped away and my father adds immortality to his list of powers?

"When do we leave?" Darius asks.

"As soon as you subdue Bernadette," Timót says, his eyes on my wand. "As a show of good faith. I need to know you're on my side before you deliver me to the king."

Darius' eyes pull away from mine for the briefest moment, glancing at my father and then returning to me. In the fraction of a second while he looks away, I feel him return to me. I feel his pain, sense his sorrow and his rage. But the sensation disappears as quickly as it comes, leaving me empty again.

"Of course," Darius says, his tone sending an ice-cold dagger into my heart. "So you're aware, the king won't trust to turn you until he sees the baby on the altar. Even then…"

My wand trembles in my hand. To hear these words from Darius' lips shreds any sense of control I have left.

You're a monster.

Hatred pushes out the pain and betrayal, leaving nothing but rage toward this man I once loved with all of my soul, who I allowed to become myself, to inhabit my very being. The anger is maddening, and it's finally pushed me too far.

"Sebhely tüz!"

I scream the first fire spell that comes to mind, one meant to maim but not necessarily to kill. A thin line of light darts out of my wand, sparks flying from the tip. As fast as the blast leaves my wand, Darius is somewhere else. It would appear vampires move faster than the speed of light, and we hadn't covered paranormal speed in my witching lessons before the attack. Poor planning, I guess.

Before I can plot my next move--having barely thought out my initial attack--I feel a burning rope wrap around my body. Timót has seized the opportunity to wrangle me, as a bright cord extends from his wand and tightly binds my arms to my sides. I look down to see my hands trapped at my thighs, my wand uselessly pointed at the stone beneath my feet.

Looks like my first instinct to keep my shit together and not lose my cool was the right call. Now I'm helpless and hopeless, with a screaming baby pinned even more tightly to my chest.

There's no longer any chance of keeping my emotions at bay, and tears roll down my cheeks and dampen Rain's little hairs. Through my blurry eyes I see Darius and Timót moving in my direction. They stand next to each other, two men who I thought were on opposite sides of this war and in opposite spectrums of my affection. Things haven't made sense for a long time now, but this is the most incomprehensible development.

"You're powerful," Timót says. "There's no question of that. But you're not prepared to fight the forces at odds with you."

"Let's go," Darius says, his black pupils looking more hollow than fierce. I don't think I even recognize this man anymore.

"Not until everyone is ready," Timót says, his eyes narrowed as he glares at the vampire. They've clearly agreed on the basics of a plan, but implicit trust is definitely lacking in this partnership.

"I don't want any foul play from the young witch. And, let me remind you," Timót says as he points his wand toward the sky, "that you're quite outnumbered."

The tip of his wand brightens, but instead of sending out a flare of light, it emits a deep, pulsing hum. The sound reverberates in my ears for a few moments, and then my eyes dart from side to side as various figures appear around us. Some wear cloaks like Timót, others are dressed in unfamiliar styles, and some don't look human at all. It's an eclectic assortment of men, now forming a circle around us and making a bad situation feel infinitely worse.

"There was no shortage in disenfranchised people and creatures wanting to join a greater cause," my father says as the strangers draw closer. "These men understand the real damage the witch's prophecy has brought. Someday you will both see what they see."

As Timót's army appears, Darius' stare never waivers from mine, though a quick blink shows me his hesitation. Whether he's trying to decide an action or swallowing his pride, I can't tell.

That momentary lapse gives me a glimmer of hope. Perhaps this is all part of a ploy--lead Timót on long enough to make him complacent, then rip him apart. After all, Darius wouldn't break a sweat killing this *Érintett* leader, I don't care how powerful he is or what army he's brought. There's no way any of these men can match the strength and cunning of the vampire prince.

The more I think about it, the more convinced I am that this is the moment my love will return to me. Timót will feel protected by his men, and that's when Darius will strike and rip his wand away. Then I'll be free to use my magic and we'll send the dragons and the *Érintett* followers running for the hills.

My hope strengthens with each second. Darius

is conflicted, but not about what to do, just how to do it. Is it really this simple? All of Timót's careful planning laid to waste by trusting the wrong vampire?

He starts to walk toward me at a slow, steady gait. He'd move faster if he meant to disarm or hurt me. The pace will allow him to pick his moment, kill the lot and carry me to safety.

Any second now, he'll move at an imperceptible speed and plunge a dagger into my father's chest. Or snap his neck. Or cut his throat.

Any second now.

Any...

Second.

Darius reaches my side, his eyes devoid of feeling as they stay locked with mine. I sense the same steady stream of anger inside him, but I can't understand where it's directed. For all I know, all the hostility could be aimed at me.

He reaches up and wraps his fingers around my wand, his cool touch passing through the piece and into my hand.

Then the sensation--and my wand--are ripped away.

He walks back to Timót and unceremoniously hands over the beautiful, rare, exquisite wand I worked so hard to make. Timót grins and slides the stick into the sleeve of his cloak.

"Thank you," he says to Darius.

The vampire nods and steps away, his gaze still on me. If his plan was to kill my father and save my child, he's just made it infinitely more difficult. As for me ever forgiving him, he's made it all but impossible.

"Now we may go. Come, my *sárkányok*," Timót says, and with a wave of his arm the dragons descend to the ground around us. All of the soldiers that were just revealed begin climbing on the beasts' backs, making it clear we're traveling as a pack. The strangers throw sideways glances at me and Rain, but I can't be bothered to pull my focus away from Darius and my father. I glance between the two, not knowing who to hate more. In their own ways, both gave me life, and now it feels like they're both trying to take that away.

Timót points his wand at me and mutters *úszó*, sending me and Rain floating a few feet above the ground. "You'll ride on Agoston, Bernadette. She's the oldest of the thunder."

I feel a warm, scaly body slither beneath me as I'm lowered onto the creature's back. Agoston is bright orange with purple markings along the edges of her wings. I wonder if she was also stolen from her mother in the deep caves.

The warm tether that had just been wrapped around my torso now snakes around my legs as well, strapping me to the dragon's back. As I study my mythical transportation, my gaze drifts back to AJ's body. I have no idea if she's alive or dead, but I can't bear to leave her either way.

"Please," I say. "Can't we save her? Or at least bring her so I can say goodbye?"

Timót, now mounted on a dark blue dragon, looks at my fallen friend, his expression skeptical. Before he can answer, Darius speaks.

"If she's not already dead, the vampires would kill her quickly. Chances of survival are better if she stays here."

We're in a different world, in the middle of nowhere, with no idea what kind of help AJ might need, and he thinks it's best to just leave her? If there had been a tiny flicker of hope left that my Darius still existed, it just got snuffed out.

He climbs onto the back of a large, green beast. With his head turned away from me, I feel his soul flash through mine. When he pauses his climb, I know he feels it as well.

Forgive me, he whispers into my mind.

Hearing his voice again almost breaks me, but my anger is a living fire raging in my soul, and it consumes my grief, using the fodder of my crushed heart as fuel for growth. He's taken us past the point of no return, and no words can fix that.

Never, I whisper back.

CHAPTER TWO

My dragon keeps to the center of the pack as we fly above the rocky, colorless landscape. I realize that the overcast skies aren't part of any weather pattern, but rather the constant of the vampire realm; the sun never touches this place. There's a huge mountain range to our left with just the slightest glow along its highest ridge. I'm guessing it's daytime on the other side, but the rays never make it this far.

Because of that, I don't see any forests or fields. No bees buzzing around flowers or birds nesting in trees. There's the occasional stream of rust-colored water running through the scarred face of the hardened ground, but otherwise the view is completely desolate.

And even that water looks less... watery... somehow. Like if you tried to drink it, it would definitely stick in your throat.

It matches my mood perfectly.

I've stopped trying to feel any union with Darius. The effort is exhausting and being stonewalled only deepens the wound in my heart. My focus now rests solely on Rain, who cried herself to sleep in the first few minutes of flight. I hum different lullabies to her, hoping to keep her resting peacefully. My poor girl has endured so much already in her short life, and it feels like the worst is still to come.

No one speaks as we fly, but I get my fair share of looks from Timót's gang. There are dwarves, giants, goblins, shifters--it's a pretty diverse spread on the backs of these dragons. The only consistency is the testosterone count; every one of them is male. They all leer at me and my baby, thinking whatever awful thoughts run through the brains of the type of men who would join this type of cause. *Hey, come with me, we're going to gain power by kidnapping my daughter and stealing her kid.* Shocking that he couldn't get any women on board.

Darius rides behind me, my sense of him ebbing and flowing as we travel. He's still distant, perhaps even more so since I stopped trying to connect with him. It's for the best, I suppose. His aloofness makes it easier to pretend he never existed.

Zev, please, I whimper in my thoughts. *Come to me.*

I wait for an answer, even though I know it's hopeless. I feel a howl inside my heart, but that's just my lonely soul crying out for its mate.

After twenty minutes or so in the air, the thunder of dragons begins to descend. We settle on another patch of gray stone, this one just as bleak and dead as every other part of these lands. On the horizon, I see the outlines of tall, angular buildings. I wonder what they look like close up, but I'm sure that question will be answered soon enough.

Timót slides off the back of his dragon and turns to face his legion, all of whom sit at various levels of attention. "Welcome to Vaemor."

The men smile, nod, some even laugh. They're excited. This is fun for them.

Gross.

"I'll venture into the temple with Darius, the mother, and the child," he says, referring to me as *the mother*, like any good father would. What a brutal parenting hand I was dealt.

"You'll hear and see activity as the Ancients head to the pantheon and prepare the altar," he continues.

"The moment you see my flare, flood the city with dragons."

The Ancients, huh? Vampires sound pompous as hell. Then again, how else do you describe old dudes who have been kicking around since the dawn of all things?

This loose outline of a plan doesn't make me feel particularly safe. Call me crazy, but attacking vampires with dragons right before my baby gets sacrificed sounds like an awesome way to get everyone killed. Especially my baby.

My father points his wand at me and does the little levitating trick, flying Rain and me off the dragon and onto the ground. I give the other dragons a quick glance, thinking about how sad they must be, and wondering how broken they are by this man. Like horses ridden by Confederate soldiers, unwittingly aiding an evil cause.

My insides slosh around like jello on a slick platter as dear ol' dad jerks me around, and I do my best to protect Rain, who starts to scream again as my feet hit the ground. She hasn't eaten in hours and, well, everything sucks. No real surprise she's fussy. It's a solidly relatable mood right about now.

"Can I feed my child?" I ask, keeping my tone

cold and my voice quiet in an attempt to stave off the hysteria that's nearly overtaking me.

Timót's face shows a trace of empathy, either completely staged or bubbling up from some hidden part of his heart that's still human. "Of course."

The cord of light loosens around us and then slithers back into his wand. My arms are stiff from being clasped against my sides for so long, but I shake it off and unstrap Rain as fast as I can to get her feeding. Wrecked as I may be, I can still give her some contentment.

As she takes the nipple and starts to drink, I'm self-conscious about the feeding process for the first time since she was born. All of these strangers stare at me, making no effort to look away or not appear to be total creeps. So far I'm really loving the company my dad keeps.

"As soon as she finishes, let's begin the walk," Timót says to Darius. I haven't given the vampire so much as a sideways look since getting off the dragon, though I can feel his eyes boring into me like icy daggers. As long as I live, which might not be much longer, I'll never understand what happened to him. Or has he always been this much of an ass, conning me into trusting him while working backroom deals?

No. There's no way. After all, he's gaining nothing

from this he didn't have to begin with. I was already pledged to him eternally, our souls fused together as one. If this has been his plan all along, he's just walking away with no baby, a fallen kingdom, and a scorned lover who wants him dead.

There has to be more to it.

Why?

I try sneaking the question in again, hoping to catch him off guard. I feel a twinge of pain from him, but nothing else. No meaningful response.

I hope Rain will feed forever so we don't have to march her into the vampire stronghold, but she pops off the breast and delivers a satisfied burp, all but announcing to my captors that she's ready to roll.

"Very good," Timót says. "Let us away to meet King Vladimir."

Darius walks briskly past me, wasting no time leading us toward the ancient temple of the vampires. This is exactly what his oath was meant to protect me and Rain from, meaning he either had his fingers crossed when he made the pledge, or magic is bullshit.

While I toil with a dismantled world and the blurred lines between fact and fiction, my father seems to be feeling more invincible by the moment. He walks in a brisk stride, strutting like he's walking into his own kingdom, not an enemy stronghold. I know he wants the strength of immortality, but I still can't fit together all the pieces of his puzzle. He's after power, but what's his strategy for getting it? What does the Last Witch mean to his efforts? What's his plan for me and my powers, especially since all I really want to do is melt him down and then pour his molten shit corpse into an ocean?

And when--Jesus Christ Almighty WHEN--did he rope in Darius? The vampire has been at my side nearly every second since we arrived in Budapest, and when he was away our souls were still connected. They've clearly had enough communication to work out a pretty involved scheme, so were they writing letters? Was it all done while I was away with Zev? Or Rune? Did it happen because I was away with another prince and Darius got jealous?

I fight the urge to search the vampire's mind for answers, because I know he'll just shut me out and hurt me more. I can only hope I get some clarity before I detonate like an atomic bomb and kill everyone. I'm not quite there yet, but I've got enough confidence in my powers to at least give it a shot when the moment arrives.

As we start down a slight incline that leads to the city, I can finally study the fascinating metropolis a bit more. The structures are very gothic, with tall points and turrets capping all the roofs. The hardest thing to reconcile is the lack of roads. One building merges into the next, with no room for vehicles or foot traffic. It strikes me as odd until I notice the vampires flashing about above the different premises. They leap and bound, grabbing hold of the erected pinnacles and then entering through horizontal doorways. I open my mind a little and it makes more sense; why travel on roads when cars would slow you down?

It doesn't take long for a few vampires to notice our arrival. One by one, figures clad in dark velvet and pristine silks begin zipping over to us, standing along the perimeter of the city while they assess the visitors. I see one vampire whisper to another, and the second is gone in a flash. If I have to guess, he's recognized Darius and is off to fetch someone with authority.

More and more vampires join the crowd until there are at least fifty, with many more watching from a distance. I wonder if every envoy receives this big a greeting party. Now that I think about it, Vaemor probably doesn't get many visitors; it's all dead, devoid of sunlight, and full of vampires. Not a lot of travelers passing through these parts, for business or pleasure, I imagine.

Excruciatingly long seconds pass in silence, with Darius and Timót in a winner-take-all staring contest with the locals. Finally, I see a figure in dark robes exit one of the taller buildings. A few deferential men walk behind him, I'm guessing they're guards or servants. He walks with another, younger man, dressed in more modern attire, gold trim lining his black coat. The closer he gets, the more handsome and stylish he appears, almost as though he could be--

"Brother."

He addresses Darius before I can finish connecting the dots. Darius doesn't say anything back, only offering a swift nod before moving his gaze to the older vampire, who can only be the king.

"You've been away for some time, my son," Vladimir says, his wrinkled face and pitchy voice the epitome of villainous. "It seemed you had strayed far from the prophecy."

"Well," Darius says, clearing his throat in that way people do when they're fighting the urge to say what they really think. "It seems there's no such thing as a tidy ending to a prophecy as old as time."

Darius' father smiles, making sure to show his long, yellowed fangs as he does. I can't imagine how many lives those daggers have taken, and I try to push the thought out of my head before I start doing any nauseating calculations.

The vampire king turns his attention to me, the hideous smile still resting on his face. "Here you are, in the... flesh." He takes his time with the last word and lets his eyes drift over my neck and down to my child. It puts me a big step closer to pulling the pin on atomic bomb Bernie.

I sense an urgency in my legs to step forward, to move closer to the monster as he looks back up from my baby and into my eyes. It's a familiar feeling, and I know immediately he's trying to compel me. I stare back at him, willing my legs to stay right where they are. I push back with my mind, fighting to compel him instead. After a few grueling seconds, the pull in my legs fades away, as does the vampire's smile.

"Hm," he says as he studies me. "I suppose I should have expected as much from a witch who is so desirable. Very good, girl. This means the blood of your child will be that much stronger."

Leaving me with that charming sentiment, the king turns to Timót and stares expectantly.

My father quickly picks up his cue. "My name is Timót. I sired the mother of the Last Witch and brokered the deal that brought her safely here. I've been promised eternal life in exchange for the child."

Vladimir quickly looks from Timót to Darius, cocking an eyebrow. "Brokered a deal, Darius? A very bold move for someone so eager to toy with treason."

As mad as I already am, I feel my blood boil a little more, and I know it's Darius that I feel. I may never understand what's driving his decision-making in all this, but it has nothing to do with loyalty to his father.

Before Darius can speak, his brother steps in on his behalf. "I think we can trust that the challenges presented have been substantial, father." The brother looks between me and Darius, trying to glean a little insight from our expressions. There's probably too much going on for him to get a clear picture.

I'm certainly clueless about half of what's happening, particularly if it involves my tratorious vampire lover.

"This is why Darius was sent and not you, Emerus," King Vladimir says with a grunt. "You try too hard to see the good. And you may have rubbed off on your brother."

Vladimir returns his attention to my father, sizing him up and weighing the bargaining chip. "Any reason not to simply kill you and take the child on my own terms?"

"Because..." It's Darius speaking up on Timót's behalf, which takes everyone by surprise. "I've made a pledge and it deserves to be acknowledged. If the vampires are saved by the blood of the child, why defy the wishes of the man who helped fulfill the prophecy in our favor?"

Darius standing up to his king father on Timót's behalf instead of fighting to save Rain causes me more pain than I thought I could feel. I was sure my senses had been bludgeoned into numbness, but apparently I still have the capacity to break further.

Vladimir sneers at Darius, then shrugs. "Very well. No use wasting time arguing with your flawed reasoning, son. Best to bring the child to the temple with haste. Emerus, fetch the Ancients. We will begin immediately. We've no time to waste."

Vladimir turns and heads back toward the city walls. Emerus lingers a second longer, looking into the eyes of his brother, then he disappears in a blur. By this time, I can see hundreds upon hundreds of the city's residents watching from the tops of their buildings. Word has spread and they're all stepping out to bear witness.

The nearest vampires follow their king, throwing

the occasional look over their shoulder to see the Last Witch. The sacrifice that will give them the power they've desired for hundreds of thousands of years.

Timót comes to my side and takes me by the arm, leading me after the pack. Before I can lash out at him for the unwanted touch, he mutters under his breath. "I'm only standing close to protect you. While the vampires don't care what happens to the Last Witch's mother, I do."

I can't fight or argue with him, because even if he doesn't give two shits about my life, he's definitely not wrong about the vampires. To them, I'm just a body waiting to be drained. I can see it in their anxious, bloodshot eyes.

"You might not want to trust me," my father goes on, "but you've heard the plan and know of my fleet. I'm your only hope for survival."

I will say this: my father is the biggest piece of shit and worst father since Cronus. He's also pretty smart and seems to have his bases covered in this impossible quest.

As we head toward the entrance of a small building, more and more vampires circle around us. It doesn't take long for me to feel a modicum of comfort having Timót by my side, which I find disgustingly ironic. The vampires don't bother to keep their distance, and I can feel some of them breathing against my neck and shoulders. I keep my arms wrapped tightly around Rain, who's thankfully fallen back to sleep.

We walk through the rounded doorway of the stone building. The entrance leads to a stairway that descends into the rocky ground, and I'm suddenly worried that Timót's plan has a giant flaw--how are we going to get a squadron of dragons underground?

The vampires lead us down the steps and into the darkness. Before we get too deep, the stairs turn into a level hallway. Looking past the people in front of me, I can see a sliver light trickling in from an opening at the end of the passage. The light gets steadier as we get closer, and at the end of the hall we step into a giant, open room. The ceiling above rounds into a dome, with an open mouth at the top, which allows me to breathe a small sigh of relief. Dragon door: check.

Then I see what stands in the middle of the space, and my breath catches again.

A large, stone slab sits in the center of a raised platform. The stone is at a slight incline, with grooves running down toward the vertical sides. Those deep creases lead to more lines, spider-webbing into a vast network that surrounds the altar.

A series of channels.

Below the altar.

For my baby's blood to drip.

Do not *let this happen,* I plead to Darius.

It's too late.

The words send a shock of horror through my body. It's not just the sentiment, but the voice that's doing the speaking.

Welcome to my kingdom. Vladimir's voice pierces my mind, cutting it open to speak as he faces me from across the room while sitting in a large, obsidian throne.

I try my best to wall off my mind, praying I'll never have to hear his thoughts again and hoping to God he's not going to keep listening to mine.

The vampires that walked into the temple with us have climbed into seats above in rafters that circle about the room. We're on a stage, everyone here to watch something abjectly grotesque.

Through an entrance at the other end of the temple, Emerus leads in a trio of men, their faces obscured by hoods. They move over to three stone benches that are stationed around the altar. I can't see their eyes, but I know each of them is staring at me. Staring at my baby.

My body jolts when two hands tightly grip my

arms. I struggle briefly to break free but it's no use. I'm no match against vampire super strength, and I feel even weaker when my boiling blood shows that the one gripping me is Darius. A touch I used to long for now pushes me closer to my deepest despair. As he holds me, I feel the straps of the baby harness loosen and fall away from Rain. Vladimir coaxes the air with his fingers, controlling her little body as she lifts from the harness and floats toward the altar. A muffled sob escapes my lips as I watch her move away from me, my heart bursting from the gut-wrenching fear that I've touched my darling girl for the last time.

I glance down at my hands to see a familiar glow building within. I'm not sure I'll be able to fend off the evil surrounding me for long, but I'm damn willing to light this place on fire and see what happens.

The moment I entertain the thought of putting my magic to use, a pair of fangs diving into my neck sucks all the air from that idea. Darius drinks away my magic, my blood, and my hope.

No, I think, perhaps not even audibly as I feel myself drain.

Wait, he says in response.

I don't know what it means, but I'm surprised to finally get any connection from him in return. Wait for what? For my child to die? That's exactly what I'm not willing to wait on.

"Do you plan to save any for the rest of us, Darius?" Vladimir's joke is met with a chorus of laughter from the gallery above. My eyes open as Darius releases me, and I see that Rain now lies flat on the stone altar, the Ancients standing about and inspecting her.

"Just keeping her powers from overwhelming and killing you, father," Darius snaps back. There's no love lost between these two, and I'm not sure why he didn't just let me burn the piece of shit to a crisp.

The Ancients move back to their benches, having completed whatever inspection needed to happen. Rain is now awake but completely still, as she looks around but makes no noise. She's still under the control of Vladimir and I know she's terrified.

Everyone's attention shifts as my sleeze of a father steps forward. "I have fulfilled my end of the agreement," he says. "Now I expect the same."

The room falls silent as Vladimir stands and approaches Timót, the vampire king taller than I realized as he towers over my father--not a small man himself.

A kind of ancient power radiates out of him, and

I bristle at the nearness of it even though he's still several feet away from me.

I try to study everything and everyone, to learn what I can that might be of use in rescuing my baby.

It's so hard to tear my eyes off her, but I know my focus should be elsewhere if I have any hope of getting us out of here.

The king leans in to speak to Timót, his voice cold and bloodthirsty. "Not everyone survives a Turning," he hisses.

To my father's credit, he doesn't flinch. He's still an ass of the highest order, but it's good to see someone standing up to Darius's super awful dad.

Looks like I'm not the only one with daddy issues.

"I'm prepared to accept any consequences of this decision," Timót says with an air of confidence that doesn't sound fake. He really believes he's going to win.

That might be the scariest part of all of this. His unwavering confidence in the face of the king of vampires.

"Very well," the ancient vampire says. "I will honor my son's word--foolish though it may be--and give you our gift that very few receive. Let us hope you are worthy."

My father just smiles, so freaking smug in his worthiness.

My heart thuds in my chest as I watch my child, praying for a way to save her before it's too late. Hating Darius for taking the only means I had of protecting us. How could he condemn us to this fate? None of this makes sense.

Vladmir's teeth extend into predatory sharpness and pierce Timót's jugular. My father's face is stoic as the vampire feeds on him, but after a few moments it's clear the blood loss is having an excruciating effect.

The color drains from his face at an alarming rate. His body is shaking, and he looks ready to collapse at any moment.

Is Vladimir going to kill my father? Like, for good?

I want him to. I want my dad to pay for what he's done with his life. At the same time, it can't happen yet. Not until he's done his part to save me and Rain from a city full of vampires.

The king lets my father fall to the ground like a sack of potatoes. I flinch, but I don't feel any sympathy for my mom's sperm donor.

I might have. Once upon a time. When I was a little girl with fantastical and silly dreams about who and what my father was. An astronaut stuck in space? A prince in exile who couldn't risk our safety by coming to us? A spy who lived a secret life?

But adulthood disabused me of those silly notions.

What I do feel is an urgent need to do something, anything, to save my daughter while the vampires are distracted by this charming ceremony.

Throwing caution to the wind, I'm about to rush the altar and take my chances, magic or no, when a crushing grip squeezes my forearm painfully.

Wait.

Again, only one word. No context. No explanation. No nothing.

This is utter bullshit.

I let out a string of expletives into his mind that would make a sailor blush as I try to yank out of his grip to no avail.

So help me god if anything happens to my child I will stake your cold, dead heart, then behead you, then burn your body and scatter your ashes to the four corners of the earth and beyond.

I feel only sadness from him, but then it's cut abruptly like a faucet being turned off.

My father moans, distracting me from my focus on Darius and back to the scene before us.

Vladmir is leaning over Timót, holding a bleeding wrist to his mouth. My father is drinking the vampire king's blood.

The two of them exchanging blood can't be enough to turn him. Darius and I have done that so many times, I'd for sure be a vampire by now if that were all there was to it.

There is more to it, the king whispers into my mind as he locks eyes with me. I clearly failed to keep that damn wall up.

He smiles in a way that's totally creepy, and then very viciously snaps my father's neck, killing him instantly.

And with that final, brutal act, the man who had been nothing more to me than a childhood curiosity turned nightmare, slumps to the ground.

I suck in my breath as Vladimir stands, his thin lips twisted into a gloating smile as he turns his attention to Rain.

CHAPTER THREE

I stand frozen in place, stunned by what has just happened. Even if Darius does loosen his grip, I won't be able to move.

"And now, the ceremony," Vladimir says.

The three eldest vampires begin to chant, softly and quietly, and the rest of the temple falls silent. Aside from the king and the Ancients, every vampire crosses their arms in an X over their chest and stares down at the ground. The uniformity of it is impressive, like they've been running daily prophecy fulfillment drills for hundreds of years. Shit, maybe they have.

Just as Vladimir takes in a deep breath, ready to launch into something terrible, Darius interrupts.

"Father, do we not first wish to bless the mother and child, as the prophecy reading would dictate. Lest we waylay our plans entirely through improper planning."

Vladimir holds up a hand, pausing the chanting. "You are quite right, son. It seems thousands of years of waiting have me acting rashly. We would be remiss in taking any shortcuts on this most auspicious occasion. Priests, bring forth the unholy waters for anointing."

Unholy waters? Oh hell no, are these dead assholes trying to give me and my kid a reverse baptism? My Catholicism has long since lapsed, but even I don't want to mess up my afterlife chances, especially with how frequently my child and I seem to flirt with death.

Two priests in long gray robes step forward holding small pewter bowls filled with--apparently--unholy water. I don't even want to know what makes water unholy. I also have questions about what makes these guys priests.

As one moves toward Rain and the other toward me, they chant together in a strange, ominous language. When each priest arrives at his mark, they draw water from the bowls and use the pads of their thumbs to paint a half circle with a dot in the center on our foreheads.

I don't expect to feel anything but annoyed, but a zing pulses in my spine, then fades, and I shudder.

What did they do to me? And more importantly, what did they do to Rain?

Darius keeps his grip on my arms, and I start to pull against him, ready to die if it means I go out trying to save my baby girl. No matter how hard I strain, he keeps me still. I doubt he's even putting in much effort.

"The mother and child are now duly blessed," Vladimir says as the priests walk back into the shadows. "We may begin."

The chanting resumes, now accompanied by a low hum from all the vampires who continue looking at the ground with their arms crossed.

I stop fighting against Darius when it's clear I'm just wasting my strength, and I turn my attention to Timót. No one else is paying any attention to my father, as he's pretty dead looking. Maybe it takes a long time for the transition to happen, or maybe all Vladimir did was kill him for good. In any case, the vampires pay Timót no mind, so when his body twitches, I'm the only one who sees it.

My eyes dart around the room, trying to gauge

where we are in the process. Vladimir still stands away from Rain, and all the vampires have intensified their humming. The vigor of the ceremony is really ramping up, as is my heartbeat.

When my eyes shift back to Timót I fight the urge to gasp as he blinks. His eyes slowly focus on me... and then he smiles.

Daddy is back, and now in addition to magic, dragons, and an army, he's also got access to all the cool vampire tricks.

He looks toward the opening in the ceiling. He has a vampire on either side of him, but they have their arms crossed and their eyes closed. To the vampires, this ceremony is about the survival of their kind, so commitment levels are very high. That makes it easy for my father to sneak the tip of his wand out of his sleeve and point it to the sky. I try to blank out my mind in case the king might be looking into my thoughts.

Fortunately, Vladimir is entirely focused on Rain, now walking toward her with a shimmering dagger in his right hand.

"From the beginning," the vampire king announces to the room, "we have been shunned by our creators, and feared by the other creations. Our powers were seen as a plight on the world, not a gift.

Our demands for respect were met with calls for our heads. No more."

He continues his slow walk toward my baby, his stare frighteningly entranced by her presence. I sneak another glance at Timót and see that his lips are subtly moving while a tiny speck of light drifts from his wand toward the open ceiling.

"The Fates gave us life in death, they created the prophecy for all to see, and now we will make our realm absolute."

At the edge of the altar, Vladimir raises the dagger over his head. The humming from the room grows louder, and a scream that has been brewing in my knotted stomach is about to leave my mouth when Timót shatters the silence.

"Excuse me," he says, getting to his feet and brushing off his knees like someone who just tripped and is apologizing for creating some commotion. A collective gasp ripples through the temple, and the rage on the king's face can be felt by everyone.

"You dare interrupt?!" Vladimir spits.

"Sorry, just woke," my father says, feigning ignorance. "Has the ceremony started?"

The king's lip curls and his disgusting fangs extend, making it clear what he wants to do to Timót. "I should have killed you the moment you arrived."

"Perhaps," dad says with a shrug. "A bit late for that now."

"There are still ways, you fool. Bring him to me!"

The vampires at either side of my father reach for Timót, but with equal deftness he steps back, grabs them by the arms and throws them to the ground. In the same instant, Darius has released me and is on top of the fallen attackers, keeping them away from Timót.

The king glares at his son, surprised and appalled by his actions. "What are you doing?"

"He's only taking precautions," Timót says, his wand aimed at the king. "As he knows what comes next."

Right on cue, an ear-piercing roar echoes through the room. All faces turn upward in time to see dozens of nose-diving dragons fly through the opening in the dome, swarming the temple.

My eyes immediately shoot back to Rain, completely exposed in the center of the chamber. Vladimir stands next to her. I see terror in his eyes as more beasts flood in through the open ceiling. As the vampire king moves out of the center of the room, I sprint to the altar, practically throwing my body over Rain in case a burst of fire is about to hit. As soon as she's wrapped in my arms, someone lifts me and starts to carry us away. I expect to see Darius, or perhaps Timót. Instead I'm shocked to see Emerus rushing me off to the sidelines. He tucks us into a small recession in the stone wall, out of the reach of the dragons and hopefully unseen by the vampires.

"The child cannot die like this."

Adding the qualifier "like this" takes away from the kindness of the gesture, but I'll take what I can get. Emerus flashes away from me, presumably to save himself.

I look above to see that Timót has mounted his dragon, but the creature stays on the ground, marching over to the three Ancients who are pinned in the corner. A few vampires run to their defense, only to be lit on fire by the scorching dragon breath. There's a strange moment where the elderly vampires seem to accept their fate and bow their heads. I wonder briefly if Timót might spare them, but that thought dies more quickly than the Ancients as a stream of fire erupts from the dragon's mouth and consumes them.

While the undead relics flail, Timót turns his attention back to the altar where Rain had been. The look on his face is one of unbridled power. His plan has worked and his life is eternal. He believes he's the most powerful man to ever grace the universe... and there's a chance he's right.

He steadies his wand and aims it at the altar--an ancient piece of stone built for the sole purpose of staging my baby's death. In this moment, I'm one-hundred-percent team psycho dad.. I want him to wreck that goddamn thing. Don't leave anything behind but dust. And then take that dust and make it more dust until it's microscopic. Then scatter that to all the worlds so this monstrosity can never be rebuilt.

"Elpusztítani teljes," he yells, and a ripple of red light bursts forward and into the stone. There's the briefest pause before the altar explodes into tiny particles, floating into the surrounding space and coating everything nearby in tiny flecks of debris.

Good goddamn riddance.

Timót gives one last look at the spot where the altar used to be, admiring his destruction, before turning back to find his next target--King Vladimir.

The vampire leader has been carefully dodging flames and alluding fighters, but making no move to escape the fray. His fangs are out, looking longer than ever, ready to kill anything that comes near.

"I'm sorry things haven't gone quite to plan, Vladimir." My father approaches the king, his dragon ready to do its worst. I wonder if someone as powerful as Vladimir might be able to survive a blast of dragon fire. The way his eyes keep jumping between Timót and the giant creature's nostrils makes me think he's not feeling too confident.

"What shall you do?" Vladimir asks. "Run off with the child? Hide away until the vampires find you? Don't think for a second that we won't."

"But whatever for?" Timót says with a laugh. "You've no altar. No Ancients to perform your rituals. Your poor interpretation of the prophecy has no chance for fulfillment."

The king snarls, taking a step closer to my father and the dragon. Maybe I was wrong about him being afraid. Maybe nothing can kill this old monster.

"Altars can be rebuilt," he hisses. "Songs from old lore can be rediscovered."

Timót nods, a pompous smile on his face.

"That's all true. Perhaps things will go exactly as you say. But you certainly won't be around to see it."

His face turns from cocky to crazed as he wrenches back on the reigns around the dragon's head and a massive swath of fire circles around the king. I watch as Vladimir stands in the fire, his body not moving. He's either invincible or welcoming death, and I won't know until the flames subside.

But that might never happen.

The dragon continues to scorch the king, moving closer as the hot blue fire wraps around the vampire. Now I can hear Vladimir's screams, though his body is unmoving. The dragon leans closer still, now practically on top of its target. Timót keeps his grip on the rains, not letting up at all.

With their faces inches apart, the dragon fire finally stops. I hold my breath as I wait to see what's become of the king, but I'm never given the chance. In one swift, gruesome motion, Timót's giant creature takes the vampire king into its mouth, its colossal teeth shredding charred flesh and crunching through old bones.

No more wondering about the vampire king.

I duck back into my hiding place as Timót looks around the room. I'm not sure how much more killing he wants to do before he starts searching for me.

The vampires have largely fled from the room. The fiery attack has forced them away, and only a few fighters remain. I glance around, looking for Darius, and while I can't see him, I feel him more strongly. I feel less anger, and a sense of calm. The timing feels odd, what with dragons everywhere breathing out fire and ending the previously endless lives of vampires.

Where are you?

I don't know why I ask, because I hate him. Still, something about the change has me wondering enough to ask. I'm not sure I'll get a response, so when I hear the words, and the voice that puts them in my brain, tears of hope and joy burst out of me.

He's with us, love. We're coming for you.

CHAPTER FOUR

Z ev.

Oh my God, Zev.

I hug Rain closer to my chest, my tears spilling onto her little head, my heart pounding through my ribs.

They're here. And Darius is with them? Confusion and anger war within me, even as an actual literal war is waging all around me.

I slink as far into the wall's recession as I can to keep my baby and myself safe. My magic is still weak from the feeding Darius did, giving me yet another reason to forgive him never. He fed to disarm me. His intention was to weaken me. As my baby lay on the sacrificial altar, he sought to make me powerless.

Wait for us. Stay safe.

Zev's voice breaks me from a spiral into despair. Having my wolf mate so close gives me hope I didn't have a few minutes ago. I can feel his presence in my mind, in my heart, and it renews my strength and helps heal a little of the pain caused by Darius.

Or at least it helps me avoid falling into pieces at the very worst possible time.

My confused and broken heart does not get to dictate my child's survival right now.

Pushing my emotional wounds to the side, I refocus on the only thing that matters: getting Rain out of here safely.

I strap her to my chest to free my arms. I need my wand, which is still tucked up the sleeve of my undead dad.

This is… tricky. He didn't want me or Rain to get killed by vampires, but only because he wants to force us to come with his weird tribe. If I go after him to get my wand, I'll probably just end up magically roped to a dragon again.

New plan. I skip the wand and get the hell out of dodge. Whatever problems arise can be figured out by future me, who will hopefully not be in the middle of getting blown up and attacked.

Though given my recent track record, that's not a guarantee. After sitting with it for a few seconds, the thought of being without my wand seems a bit calamitous.

I frantically review my options again--hoping something new pops out that makes this an easier decision--as I wait to see what Zev and the others are planning. Taking in the scene around me only makes things worse.

Above are fire breathing dragons.

Within are bloodthirsty vampires.

Without... is a desolate, dry land no human can survive.

Somehow I have to get back to my own world.

If there's a portal here, there must be one back.

Unless Zev has a better plan.

I'm really hoping Zev has a better plan.

Zev? I ask, the desperation and fear I feel bleeding into even my mental voice.

We've got a plan, love. Stay where you are. I'm coming for you.

He's coming for us. I kiss Rain's head and slink further into the shadows. It feels too passive, and part of me wants to dive into the fray and kick some ass. But without any control over my magic, I'd be the one getting my ass kicked.

Even with the wand, it'd be a tough round that wouldn't leave me unscathed. If it were just me, that'd be one thing, but… I look down at my child and my entire soul fills with a raw need to protect this small being. This little person I love more than life. More than myself. More than anything in this universe or beyond.

The feeling of that love fills me so completely that it warms me from within.

It takes me a moment to realize it's not just love that's filling me.

Rain is glowing, her skin a shimmering pearl in the darkness.

And so is mine.

My magic is ramping back up at an alarming rate. Shit.

Back to Plan A. I need to get my wand back.

Zev, I'm turning into a night light. I need to move.

He lets out a protective growl. *I'm almost there.*

I look down at my hands and shake my head. *We don't have time.*

It's not just the lightning storm exploding under my skin, but the fact that I'm a glowing target for anyone who wants to find me or Rain. And our enemy list is pretty long.

I have to move. If Zev can track me this far, a hundred more yards shouldn't present a problem. I need to find my father and get these powers under control.

No more accidentally burning down ancient groves or singing people I love.

I worked too hard to get my wand to come back to this again.

I dart out of the nook I've been sheltering in and scan the area, looking for my father and trying to avoid being seen, which seems mostly impossible at this point. I'm the only glowing witch in the joint.

It takes my eyes a moment to adjust, with smoke billowing, fires burning, dragons screeching, people on both sides screaming, yelling, dying.

But it's clear which side is holding stronger. Which side is sustaining fewer casualties. Which side will walk away the victor.

My father's side. And there he is, riding above it all on his stolen dragon, his wand out, his eyes surveying the carnage.

"The Eternal Night of the Ancients is over!" My father screams, to cheers from his army, even as they continue to slaughter the remaining vampires. By the body count, many have fled or been killed. Only a few remain, scrambling away from the flames, trying to take one last life before they die for real.

"It is a new era!" he says to another round of hoots and hollers.

I see my wand, the tip just visible at the edge of his sleeve, though I have no way of reaching him while he's on a dragon. I need him to notice me and come.

A thought occurs to me, though it seems too easy. But what if?

I focus my attention on my father, trying to catch his eye. If the king could get into my mind, and so can Darius, maybe Timót can as well? Can I get his attention? I don't love the idea of bringing him into my head, but if it helps me lure him somewhere discreet where I can retrieve my wand, then it's worth it.

Father. Can you hear my thoughts? Father? I'm in danger. I need my wand or I'll lose control and destroy us all. Help!

It doesn't take much in the way of acting to inflect my plea with sufficient desperation and need. I have both in spades at the moment. But it still makes me cringe to ask for his help.

Though technically I'm just insisting he return what he stole from me.

His head jerks and I can see that he heard me, or at least sensed my presence.

When his eyes land on mine, I know he got my message.

Help.

I say it again, to hit that note a little harder. When he directs his dragon down toward me, I turn and run back into the tunnels so none of the remaining vampires or *Érintett* will see us.

I have to trust that Timót will follow me and he'll try to keep us safe.

Fortunately, I'm like a walking LED bulb. My father had to have noticed and will assume something's wrong.

I squat in the corner of an empty hall with Rain, hiding in a carved out nook and waiting for Zev and Timót to find us. Time seems to pass in slow motion, and I resist the urge to crawl out and go looking for one or both of them.

They can each find me. I will wait.

Bullshit. My skin is getting hot enough to melt my baby, I'm not waiting for anyone.

Just as I start back toward the main room, Timót arrives on foot and alone, the halls too narrow for his dragon to pass through.

As I'd hoped.

I hold out my hands, giving him a good look at my skin, at the electricity zapping through my fingers.

"I'm not safe. To her or you or anyone here. I need my wand back."

He cocks his head and smiles. "Look at you. So much raw power and you don't even know what to do with it. This is why we are the perfect team." His eyes glow with a maniacal light that does nothing to win me over. "I can help guide that power. I've had to work harder than most to cultivate my magic, and I can teach you how to tap into it, how to use it to create a better world."

"A better world? For who?" I bite my tongue before I say more. I still need my wand, and getting him pissed off at me isn't the way to make that happen.

He pulls the wand out of his pocket, and my whole body responds, lurching forward almost involuntarily, desperate to hold it, to channel my magic into and through it.

"This is a crutch they gave you to weaken you. You should let your power out!"

This isn't the direction I was expecting the conversation to go and my stomach sinks when I realize what he wants from me.

He doesn't know that getting it could kill him as well.

Maybe he thinks he's invincible now, and he

largely is. But as he's just seen, vampires have vulnerabilities. The fire released from my magic could take him out lickity split.

As my hands snap, crackle and pop, I hold them out and toward him, pushing the intention of my powers toward my father. Magic shoots out of my hands, uncontrolled, and flies everywhere, in all directions. Nothing in this hall is flammable but a rug hanging on one of the walls, and it catches fire instantly, nearly singing my father who has to step to the side to avoid getting burned.

Instead of being scared, he claps.

"Don't you see, Bernadette? We can tap into this and become the most powerful sorcerers the world has ever seen."

"We?" I ask.

He nods. "Of course. Ever since I felt my first surge of power, I've studied the witch's ability to transfer and share magic. You don't have to bear this burden alone. If you only allow me to help, together we could do great things."

My stomach clenches at his words. He wants to steal my magic.

"Sorry, I've already had my powers stolen once this lifetime. That's quite enough."

He frowns. "I would not be stealing your magic.

Only helping to give it focus. You would still be the most powerful witch in the world."

"I need my wand," I say, skipping the argument. "Please."

I hold out my hand as another random lightning burst shoots out and hits his right shoe, burning the leather with a hiss.

I'm close. Zev's voice is a reassurance I can't let show on my face.

I just need to keep Timót focused on me.

"You don't need it. You just think you do," he says, frustrating me beyond comprehension. Thanks for the mansplain about my own powers, dad. Just give me my damn wand. I work hard not to let him hear my thoughts, though, since I'm still playing the nice game.

As I open my mouth to plead some more, my wand suddenly travels from Timót's hand to mine. My look of surprise is matched by my father's, and the flurry of activity in my blood tells me a certain vampire I know has joined the conversation.

Darius moves in a blur and stands beside me, his mind still shuttered, but this time I feel regret and pain and sadness. I can't let myself soften or think about him. Not yet. Not while everything is still so volatile.

Instead, I channel all my hurt, all my rage, all my fear and pain into my wand and point it at my dad. "Call off your men, father. Release your dragons and surrender. I have every right to kill you here and now, and unless you beg forgiveness and then try to right some of your wrongs, I will."

My father laughs, which is not at all the reaction I was hoping for. "Dear girl. You're still not seeing straight. In that case, I'll take what's mine by rights and go. You'll change your mind eventually."

He whistles and the stone walls around us begin to shake, the rocks cracking as dust falls around us.

I try to take cover, but it's impossible to find anywhere that's safe. It feels like the entire structure is collapsing.

As the ceiling begins to crumble and stone falls in large chunks around us, a dragon pushes through the rubble and my father grabs hold and mounts.

I scream and begin shooting him with my wand, aiming all that pent up magic his way, but he calmly flicks his wand and creates a protective shield that deflects my blast.

As I continue my attack, his dragon blows fire between Darius and myself, sending us diving in opposite directions. I hit the ground, understanding his intention--he's slowly separating us with uncrossable lines of fire.

Darius' mind breaks open, his fear for my safety palpable. *Bernie!*

His panic spurs me to move, and I leap away from a wall just as it falls. Enormous columns are crashing to the ground and light from the sky above has started peeking into the dark halls. This ancient chamber isn't going to last much longer.

I feel Zev in my mind, and Rune's calming presence nearby. I know they're all here, but the fire separates us. I can barely hear anything over the sound of walls crumbling and dragons screeching. It's hard to see or breathe with smoke burning my eyes and choking me. I cover Rain loosely with my shirt and try to block the worst of it.

With all my senses a jumbled mess, I'm taken off guard when my father rushes me with his dragon, zapping the straps to my child carrier and swooping by to grab her from my arms.

The girth of the dragon knocks me back, and I stumble to the ground as my baby is wrenched away from me. Giant gusts of wind send dirt and ash into my face as the dragon pumps its mighty wings, lifting higher, taking my daughter further from my arms.

"No!"

I react without thinking, jumping to my feet and pointing my wand at the ground.

"Dob val vel tűz!"

A blast of light shoots into the stone beneath my feet, propelling me like a rocket toward the flying beast above. When it comes to saving Rain, I will not hesitate to turn myself into a missile.

The jolt of magic launches me at a horrifying speed, giving Timót no time to get away. When it's within reach, I hold my wand between my teeth and grab the harness around the dragon as tightly as I can, then start pulling myself up toward Rain, tucked tightly under my father's arm. I'm reminded of how horrified I was when my car seat back home would jiggle slightly, and now she's unsecured on a dragon a hundred feet in the air.

Timót's focus is forward, not having expected me to fly at him. I didn't really expect it either, but here I am, inches away from taking my child back.

As my hand finds her leg, Timót notices the stow-away on his dragon.

"How in the name of--"

Everything happens so quickly. I let go of the harness while pulling Rain free from my father's grip. As we start to fall back, I unleash everything I have into my father, blasting him directly in the chest. I

don't use an incantation or try to summon a particular spell, I just shoot pure energy into this man and
pray that it hurts.

Then I scream.

And we fall.

I look up into the sky, no idea how far the ground
is below me, no idea when I'll feel the crushing
impact as my body connects with stone.

I wrap my body around my daughter, fearing
what will happen next.

In trying to save her, I have killed us.

And then my body hits... but it's not the rocky
floor I expected.

Strong arms wrap around me, pulling me close as
our momentum changes from straight down to a new,
lateral, safe trajectory.

I squeeze my eyes closed, clutching Rain, tears
leaking onto my cheeks.

All anger is gone, for the moment at least, as the
familiar voice settles into my mind once more.

I'm sorry.

Darius... my thought trails off as I feel the
motion stop and we come to rest on the solid earth. I
look down at Rain, her eyes open and yet she's
somehow not crying. Either she's scared stiff or she's
getting too used to almost dying.

I look up from her and into the face that I'd come to love, then come to hate, and now can't understand.

Darius stares back at me, his dark eyes flooded with sorrow, remorse, and relief. Looking into those striking eyes, it's clear he thought he might lose me.

We hold eye contact a moment longer, then Darius drops to a knee.

And weeps.

CHAPTER FIVE

I stare at Darius knelt before me, head bowed, body trembling as he sobs. The sight stirs up a mix of empathy and apathy within me. My feelings are too conflicted for my own good, but one thing I am super sure of is that I'm tremendously relieved Rain is okay and I'm still alive.

I look to the sky and sigh with relief as I watch the dragons fly away. They started their departure as soon as Timót grabbed Rain, and now the massive fleet is headed off without the baby they did all this for.

Even at this distance, I can see the limp body of my father riding side saddle on his dragon. I'm under no illusions that I've killed him, but ecstatic that I at least knocked him out. I wonder how far they'll get before realizing their leader is unconscious.

With or without my baby, their victory isn't contested. In one vicious and bloodthirsty stroke, the *Érintett* crushed their fiercest opponent. The Ancients are nothing more than ash, and their king rots in the belly of a dragon.

I shake with rage as I think about how close he came to getting Rain as well.

After how close she came to dying on that altar.

And it's all because Darius betrayed me.

He slowly looks up from the ground, his face soaked with tears. My eyes bore into his, and though a big part of me just wants to kiss and hold him, I take a small perverse pleasure in the pain I see in his eyes.

My rage takes a momentary respite when I see Zev through the flames, his eyes frantically searching for me. When his gaze locks on mine, it's magnetic. He leaps through the fire in a move that forces my heart to skip a beat, and then is by my side, our mate bond like a pulse I can feel in every inch of myself.

He grabs me brusquely and wastes no time kissing me. It's a brief, passionate kiss, then he pulls away to look at my baby. He kisses Rain's head and whispers to her. "You're the bravest little girl in the world."

His words make my lips twitch into an almost-smile sprung from a grateful mom heart. How I've missed my wolf in all this chaos.

I nearly jump out of my shoes when Rune lands by Zev's side, having leapt over the fires to be near me. He's clearly seen his share of battle in recent minutes, his elvish clothing stained with soot and blood.

My vision blurs at the sight of my beautiful fae, and he immediately cups my face, sending waves of calm through both me and Rain, who pauses her sniffling to look at the man who's taken such good care of her.

I'm reluctant to give her to anyone, to ever release her from my own arms, but I must. "Will you check her? Make sure she's okay? See if anything's wrong, aside from her desperate need for a bath and bed."

Zev grunts. "We could all do with a rinse."

Rune nods and gently lifts the child from my arms, and responds to my unspoken concern. "I'll look her over, but be assured, she has a strong constitution. She's a powerful witch in her own right."

I hope that's true. I need it to be true.

Our little tribe is complete again... except for AJ. I try to hold off thinking about my friend, because I know if I give into the grief I'll never stop. I can't go there yet, not when there's so much to say. To do. Too many questions to ask.

But I'm shaking, and the adrenaline that got me through this is fading fast.

Darius, somewhat reconnected to me but still so distant, lifts me into his arms and starts walking me through the rubble.

"Put me down."

He ignores me, and Zev chuckles. I glare at the wolf. "You want to be on my shit list too?"

He shrugs. "You should hear him out, Bernie. He deserves that at least."

We climb out of the wreckage, Rune carrying Rain, who looks content in his arms, Darius carrying me--a definitely not content expression on my face--and Zev scanning the area for any remaining vampires looking for one last fight.

I have half a mind to scream at Darius now, but I'm exhausted and he's saving me the trouble of climbing out of this mess, so I keep my mouth shut and just think angry thoughts. I'll have my time to lay into him, once we get to wherever he's taking me.

We finally reach the outer walls of the chamber, only half of which still stand. A doorway leads us into a small sitting room, probably an old waiting area. It's dusty and I can still smell the burning coming from the main hall, but this place at least has a few benches where we can sit. The moment Darius puts me down, I step away from him and channel all my anger and rage. Pulling out my wand, I aim it at him, the tip pulsing silver like the fallen star it is, waiting to deliver a high-octane spell.

"You betrayed us," I say. A part of me knows he must have had a reason, but I'm too angry to want that reason, too angry to willingly forgive him.

Darius doesn't defend himself. He sits on a bench, staring back at me.

I see the pain in his eyes and feel it in my soul, and it breaks me just a little.

With a sigh, I sit next to him.

Rain and Zev have moved off to the corner to tend to my poor child and stand guard. Darius and I are left alone to talk.

I lower my wand, not from lack of anger, but my arms feel too heavy. My body hurts now that all the fighting is done. I glance to Rain, who is taking a potion from Rune. Good. She must have felt the shock of everything too.

Darius examines me with his dark gaze, then uses his teeth to slit his wrist open. "Drink. It will heal you and help repair our bond. You will see everything I did."

"What do you mean, 'repair'?" I spit back. "What happened to it?"

"I broke it," he says plainly. "And then I did my best to compel you out of my mind once we arrived in Vaemor. I needed you to feel betrayed. Now drink so you can understand."

Mission accomplished on the betrayal, I think loudly. He doesn't flinch, just keeps his wrist outstretched for me.

The red viscous liquid pools on his pale flesh, and I finally cave. I need to know. I can't keep letting this hurt in my heart fester.

I make sure he knows I'm still angry as I take his wrist to my mouth.

The moment his blood touches my lips, the last of the walls between us crumble and I fall into his memories.

Darius is with Erzsébet. It's during the battle in the Grand Hall. They're speaking privately, in a corner enclave. I see everything as though I'm perched on Darius' shoulder, almost seeing from his point of view but still aware of him.

"She can't know," the witch says. "Any insight she takes from your mind will only make things harder."

Darius' lips tighten. "This will hurt her."

Erzsébet glares back. "So will being dead or

watching her daughter die. It is the only way." She hands him a small vial, amber liquid steaming within.

He hesitates, then takes it from her and pours it into his mouth.

A long moment passes before anything happens, but then he drops to his hands and knees and cries out in such despair it nearly breaks my heart. Through our bond I can feel the intense agony he's in as the potion rips through his body, shredding his mind and soul. Blood seeps from his eyes, nose and ears, and his skin glows red like it's about to catch on fire. The longer I watch, the duller the feeling becomes for me. I know he's suffering this concoction as a way to weaken our bond.

Seeing his pain, I can't help but let out a sob. A hand reaches for me, and I realize his present self is now with me in the vision.

Keep watching, he says to my mind.

Though my heart feels like it's being ripped out of my chest, I do as he asks.

Eventually, the vampire recovers enough to stand, but his eyes are alight with the horror of what he's undergoing and his voice is laced with pain as he speaks. "I'll find Timót now and ensure they escape safely. But I'll have to leave you all to fight this battle without me. I won't leave Bernie alone a second longer than I must."

The witch queen nods. "I wouldn't have it any other way. We'll survive, and I'll watch your every move through the crystals. We'll come to you as soon as the moment is right. Just keep the mother and child safe."

Darius holds a fist to his heart. "On my life. I will not let what happened to Cara happen to Bernie and Rain."

Erzsébet's face flinches briefly at the mention of her dead daughter, and my heart newly aches for her after nearly losing my own child twice in a matter of minutes.

With that, Darius flashes away from the queen. My mind starts to return to the present moment, but Darius' pulls me back into his memory.

There's more you must see.

The image blurs, and now we're in the cemetery above the tomb where we spent so many nights. It's dark and quiet outside, probably early in the morning, just before dawn. Darius and Erzsébet walk slowly between the tombstones.

"Is there no other way?" Darius asks, though it's clear he's resigned to his task.

"We have two active threats we can't contain," she

says. "Vampires, fae and wolves will continue coming after us, and Timót has amassed power beyond what I ever could have imagined."

"How do you know?" Darius asks.

A worried look comes over Erzsébet's face. "Dragons."

Darius stops walking. The queen stops as well, turning to face him.

"There had been stories and signs for years, but no explanation. Dragonlings gone missing and mothers found dead. At first we assumed it was just the unbalance in the magical kingdoms, but then Bernadette spoke of the broken egg in the cave where Timót had gone."

"You think he's trying to build some kind of dragon army?"

"I think he's already built it, Darius." Erzsébet's words have great weight, and the vampire clearly feels it.

"He means to kill the vampires," Darius says, and I can almost see the images of his home and family dancing through his mind.

Erzsébet nods. "He wants a throne for himself, and he'll destroy anyone who might hold him back. Vampires pose the most immediate threat."

"Then why should I lead him right where he wants to go?"

"So that he'll take the bait," the queen says. "We must move this fight to a new realm, if not we'll just watch more people die. Also, I believe you can lure Timót with an offer few others can make."

Darius raises an eyebrow, unsure of what bargaining chip Erzsébet refers to.

"You're the vampire king's son," she says. "If Timót will promise Bernadette to you, you can offer him the eternal life only your father can grant. A man like Timót could not refuse such a proposal. But..."

She stops, the creases in her brow becoming deeper as a look of concern takes hold.

"But...?"

"But Bernadette can't know. Should everything go exactly to plan, it will still be incredibly dangerous. She wouldn't agree to take such risk with her child, even if it is the only path forward. You'll have to force her to go along. And she'll have to think you've broken your pledge."

Before I can fully process the exchange, I'm thrust back into Darius' memory from the fight in the Grand Hall. He's now face to face with my father, standing in the shadows only feet from the doorway that led us to the room of portals. Darius holds a frightened looking Andor by the arm.

"I've kept him safe, now do what you must and get everyone out of here before the vampires find you," Darius says.

Timót points his wand at Andor's face, mutters his spell and I watch the man shift into Rune. Seeing everything that preceded that treacherous moment is really hard to stomach.

"You've made a wise choice, Darius," Timót says as the spell takes hold of his protegé. He then hands Darius the infamous pendant, which I now understand to be a mobile portal forged with dark magic.

Darius nods, and I'm back to sensing our slackened bond, which reminds me of the potion that caused him so much pain.

"I'll see you, Bernadette, and the child on the other side."

With those parting words we pull out of the memory, both left with our blood boiling as we consider the events that brought us here. I can feel that Darius hates my father with a passion that is fierce and protective, and his love for me and Rain is all-encompassing. He would do anything for us. Even this.

Even the thing that he feared would ruin our relationship.

As long as it kept us safe.

I'm silent for a moment as I stare into the face of a man I love, but still feel so hurt and confused by. "So you led my father to massacre your people?"

He looks at the floor, searching for a good answer. "The fight was bound to bring me here. Once I pledged myself to you, I pitted myself against my family, my ancestors, and my laws. I'm not proud of what happened here today, but Timót would have come with or without my help. This way, I could make every effort to protect you."

His explanation makes sense, but the feeling I had when he took Rain... When he took my wand... When he took my magic...

It could have gone so badly.

It almost did.

I know. He says silently. *I know I hurt you. But please know I never betrayed you. Or us. I did what I did to save you. I knew we couldn't fight Timót and the vampires at the same time. Frightful as this plan was, King Vladimir will never again send assassins to find your child. Still, I'm eternally sorry.*

"I understand," I say, speaking out loud. I leave it

at that, too drained by the day and these revelations to unpack any more of my emotions.

Darius acknowledges those feelings and stands to leave me in peace. I want to reach out to him, longing to feel the love between us that was once so strong, but then another memory rocks me to my core and my anger surges again.. "What about AJ? We left her for dead."

He turns to me. "I would never leave your best friend for dead," he says softly.

"But… I saw you. I asked you. We just left…"

"Vampires have a pretty strong sense of when something is alive or dead," he says. "Her heart was strong and I knew Erzsébet was watching."

Erzsébet is with her now.

Zev's voice chimes into my mind, making my heart go a flutter for two reasons. First, his voice just does that to me, and second, my AJ is okay.

I drop to the ground and cry my freaking eyes out, letting every bit of needless mourning pour out of me. I've been fighting for my life, pushing away any thought of AJ being dead but knowing that a huge piece of my heart might be gone. Now I know she's alive and I'm just letting it all flow.

As I flood the small room with my tears, Zev's strong hands grip my sides and lift me from the ground. I'd love to keep crying, but I also have been longing for a deeper embrace with my wolf.

I bury my face in his chest and relish in his hug. The safety. The warmth. The comfort of it. Even as I do, I feel Darius on the other side of the room, his emotions and thoughts nudging against mine, and I know I will have to fully absolve him eventually. I won't be able to live with my own mind if I don't. And he did everything for us. As close as it brought us to death, we're still here.

"WILL AJ and Erzsébet come to us?" I ask as I reluctantly pull out of the hug with Zev. As much as I long for his touch, I'm giddy at the thought of being reunited with my dearest friend who's been through so much because of me.

"We'll have to see," Rune says, finally stepping forward to join the conversation and holding a baby that somehow looks clean and content. Where the shit did he find a fresh diaper? "Before we can safely-_"

Rune abruptly stops talking, his eyes on Darius. I look to the vampire as well, who stands near the door, a serious look on his face as though he's lost in thought. A few seconds of silence pass, then he looks at me.

"I need everyone to stand behind me but stay close."

"Why? What's happening? Where are we going?"

Darius puts his hand on the large, marble door handle, listening through the stone for sounds I definitely can't hear.

"They're waiting," he says. "It does us no good to stay hidden away."

"What's our plan?" Zev asks.

The four of us exchange looks, and the haunting realization that we're still in the vampire kingdom washes over us. We're surrounded by angry survivors without a plan of action, and companions of a prince who just brought death and destruction to his own doorstep.

"I don't want to force you to fight," I say to Darius. Pledged to me or not, I can't ask this man to kill more of his brethren.

"I don't know if we'd win a fight at this point, without the dragons flying overhead," Darius says.

"Can we get them on our side?" I pose my question to Darius, but I'm happy for anyone in the room to answer. "Help them see our cause?"

The moment the words leave my mouth, I realize

how important they are. The Sexies see it on my face. "That's it," I whisper.

The three princes look at each other, not yet as sure of my epiphany as I am.

"You all believe the prophecy is bogus, right?" I say to a chorus of nods. "Then that's what we have to do. We can't fight everyone. We have to make them understand that--"

"That the Last Witch is more important alive than dead," Rune says, finishing my thought with a little artistic license. "She can save us all, or fall into the *Érintett's* hands and save none of us."

This is the only path forward. Timót's army is too big, his dragons are too fierce, his magic is too powerful. If we want to stand a chance, we need a united realm.

I can feel in my lovers that they know I'm right.

Without another word, Darius opens the door and we all walk out. I grip my wand, terrified of what might come for us. Rune keeps Rain held tight against his chest, putting her safety above his own, as always. Zev stays right beside Darius, prepared to fight and die for his old friend.

As we move into the open air, climbing on top of the fallen debris from the earlier battle, there's no immediate threat. No vampires jump out at us. I don't hear any sounds from them as we step out, and I'm not sure what Darius was listening to earlier.

When we move a little higher, climbing up the fallen columns, the scene becomes more apparent.

I thought most of the vampires died in the attack.

I clearly underestimated their numbers.

Hundreds of them stand on top of buildings and fallen structures, staring down at us as we emerge.

No one looks to attack. No one even moves.

Except for one vampire, who slowly walks toward us, coming out of the rubble that was once a sacred chamber.

It's Emerus.

And he's carrying King Vladimir's crown.

CHAPTER SIX

It's not so much that we're out-numbered. I mean we are, greatly so, with vampires on every rooftop and some certainly lurking unseen in the shadows.

That's not what scares me. We've been outnumbered before, and if there's one thing I trust my powers to do, it's light shit on fire. The vampire's greatest weakness is my greatest strength. The numbers don't scare me.

It's the volatility.

It's the fragility of this shaken realm, and the realization that just hit me like a ton of bricks.

We need them.

Every last one of them.

Timót's army flies on the backs of enormous, unbreakable flame throwers. He has countless men following his lead, and I'm confident he has even more fighters waiting back at a camp somewhere. Now he has the strength and durability of a vampire. He's all but invincible.

I've spent the last few weeks wondering if I'd be on the run for the rest of my life, trying to raise my child in hidden chambers while a council of paranormals chased us down. In an instant, that's all changed. I don't want to run from these vampires, and I don't want to kill them--even if that's what they want to do to me.

I want to convince them to join us.

Emerus leaps off a crumbling wall, landing gracefully in front of his brother. He and Darius stand just a few feet apart, staring at each other in silence. Given the stakes of this showdown, I have to keep reminding myself that these are two brothers who just lost their father.

Darius has his own issues to sort out with the king's death, but it's nothing he won't recover from. With Emerus, I don't know anything about their relationship. I don't know if he saw his maker as a despicable, murderous monster, or the head of state who helped promote the best interests of his kind. I guess we'll find out soon enough.

"I know why you came, brother," Emerus says,

keeping his voice diplomatic while his balled fists show he's ready to throw diplomacy out the window if need be.

"I don't believe you do," Darius responds. He's calm and collected. A face-off with his brother could be violent and scary, but now that he's done fake-betraying me it's clear he feels a sense of relief.

"No? I understand how pledges, bonds, and oaths work." Emerus gets a little more oomph in his voice after each word, the anger starting to peek through. "I can smell your blood bond a mile away. I read your thoughts even as you tried to keep them from her, and if our father's mind wasn't so poisoned with anger over you leaving, he would have seen through you as well."

Darius looks at his feet, flashing back to those moments when he was still shunning me, moments I now know nearly crushed him. I'll have scars from those heartbreaking hours, but I'm positive the vampire's wounds will take even longer to heal.

"Then I'm lucky," Darius says. "We're all lucky. If the king saw through me and killed Bernie, we'd all be dead. That *Érintett* army would have murdered every last one of us, but the goal was to keep the mother and child alive."

"He killed hundreds! And had we sacrificed the child--"

"It would have done nothing!" Darius spits as he yells back, as impassioned as I've ever seen him get regarding the prophecy. He climbs past his brother, standing atop a chamber wall so he can address all the vampires, most of whom are probably just waiting for Emerus to give them the cue to attack this traitor.

"Don't you see? There's no sense in the prophecy, written by the Fates themselves, if the final act is to kill the last of their kind." Darius lets his words hang while the angry crowd considers what he's said. "The battle for magic and power has led us here, with three races at each other's throats and one nearly killed off, and the baby's blood would do nothing to change that."

Darius looks over the faces of the men and women he's addressing; some seem thoughtful, others still too scorned to listen. I don't know if he's expecting a response from the masses, but Emerus leaps up to the same platform to make the conversation more intimate again.

"A simple explanation from a man with simple, compromised intentions," Emerus says.

And thus the stalemate continues, the two brothers arguing two different truths. Unfortunately, the one on my side is viewed as the treasonous son and has an uphill battle if he wants to get anyone on his side.

"I suppose," Emerus says, finally breaking the silence, "that you plan to assume the throne. Perhaps your standing as the eldest heir made the decision to lead all these foreigners into our kingdom easier."

"I meant only to save the child and her mother," Darius says back, his voice barely above a whisper. "I didn't kill our father."

"His blood certainly colors your hands more than it does mine."

Again Darius' eyes scan the waiting vampires, like he's weighing their loyalty to the throne against their loathing of him.

"I'll put it in the hands of the citizenry, Emerus."

Everyone in earshot freezes, listening intently to see if Darius actually means what he said. I'm as on edge as anyone else; putting his future in the hands of those who hate him most seems like a foolhardy move. I'd speak up and tell everyone Darius has been huffing glue and doesn't know what he's talking about, but I've admittedly been a few steps behind the clever vampire for a number of days.

Emerus looks more skeptical than surprised, trying to determine his brother's angle.

"There are no Ancients to oversee a vote," he says.

"I'm aware," Darius responds.

"Nor any priests to sanctify the outcome."

"As I said, this is a decision for those who remain. Unprecedented times call for unprecedented measures." With great trepidation, Darius raises a hand and places it on his brother's shoulder. "You know I'm torn, and you know exactly why. I believe there's a life for our people beyond this prophecy. I'm willing to stake my life and my throne on it. But I won't force anyone to bend to my will."

It's as good a speech as I've heard in a long time, but I'm pretty biased. I don't imagine vamp bro will be as quick to let vamp boy slide as I normally am.

To my happy surprise, Emerus reaches a hand up and clasps his brother's. The two share a moment, perhaps trading thoughts back and forth, perhaps just embracing the mutual respect they have for one another. I don't get anything concrete through my shared thoughts with Darius, only a strong sense of adoration.

"We must duel," Emerus says, his words throwing ice water on the tender moment.

"I know," Darius says back, his response nearly knocking the wind out of me.

What? Why? I fling my questions into Darius'

mind without a care for whatever other thoughts he's dealing with. We've all nearly died too many times already to be waltzing into an extra, avoidable fight.

Emerus stares at me with a penetrating gaze. It's immediately clear he was privy to my thought exchange with Darius. "If I may be so bold... please stay out of this."

With that, he turns to face the throngs of vampires, all anxiously awaiting word from someone who will claim to be their leader.

"You need a trustworthy king. Darius and I will fight for that title. To the Pit!"

The crowd breaks into a strange, guttural chant as the brothers turn and walk back toward the center of the city.

SINCE DAY IS night and death is life for vampires, it makes sense that up is also down. The Pit stands at the highest point in Vaemor, with long columns rising from the buildings below to support the open-air arena. There's no raked seating like in a normal stadium--everyone just forms a circle, crowding around and elbowing through to get a better view of the spectacle.

I don't want to watch. I think, all things considered, this is a stupid plan. If Darius dies, the vampires will try to make quick work of me and my child. If he lives, there's no reason to assume that will turn him into a respected leader. It feels like a lose-lose.

Zev and Rune stand as close to me as possible, each holding an arm and standing their ground to make sure we don't get trampled by the restless vampires behind us. We walked close behind Darius and Emerus on the way over so now we have front-row seats, but that means we've got hundreds of vampires pushing at our backs.

I never liked mosh pits.

I keep my wand at the ready, trying to think of the spells I've learned and which would be best for stopping angry throngs of vampires coming from all directions. So far I'm drawing a blank.

Darius and Emerus have shed their cloaks and tunics. Their matching chiseled frames are a sight for sore eyes, but my mind and body are a little too weary to care about sexy visuals. I have to figure out how this is going to end, because I don't think Darius is looking that far ahead.

All this work tricking me and Timót to keep us alive, and now he might throw it all away because he's so goddamn alpha.

The look in his eyes is one I haven't seen before.

As he stands opposite his brother, both with their hands clasped in a prayer position, there's a devoutness in his aura. He might not put stock in the prophecy, but he still believes in some of the vampire ways and traditions.

Like fighting one's brother to the death to pick a new king.

I'd admire his steadfastness if it wasn't so stupid.

There has to be another way, I say into his mind.

Perhaps, he says back. *If you know what it is, please let me know.*

I'm in no mood for sarcasm, but I can't fault him the attitude. There isn't an easy answer to any of our problems, and asking the guy on the verge of battle to come up with an alternate plan isn't really fair.

A female vampire stands on the opposite side of the Pit from us, carrying a blood-red pillow that supports the crown. It looks made of pure gold with rubies embedded like blood drops around the base and pointed spikes framing it.

I turn to Zev, hoping to get a little peace of mind. "Is Darius the better fighter?"

Zev's green eyes bounce between the royal vampire brothers, sizing them up before he answers.

"I think they're fairly equal."

Not exactly what I wanted to hear.

"It comes down to motivation," Zev continues. "Darius fights for you and your child, Emerus for his kingdom. It should be an impressive match."

Impressive match? I'm sorry, are we at a sporting event, or does the existence of all things hang in the balance of who wins or loses this fight? These paranormal princes seem to take cataclysmic events in stride and it's making me feel insane.

Fortunately, sweet Rune has a better hold on how emotions work. His touch pours calming energy into my veins, quieting the disturbed sensation I get from Darius' blood.

"I think Darius has something his brother lacks," the fae whispers to me. "Breaking his bond with you over the last day was a fate worse than death for him. I don't think he's ready to lose you again."

I take a little bit of comfort in that, though my confidence still wanes a bit.

"How…" I try to think of a delicate way to word my question, but there isn't one. "How do they kill each other?"

Rune takes a breath, and he's either trying to remember how it works or searching for an answer that won't make me cringe. Again, no such answer exists.

"By either ripping off the other's head or taking out the other's heart."

Perfect.

Any sense of calm I had disappears right away as my mind starts reeling for another option beyond the fight. I'm not sure how long I have before the duel begins, but hopefully--

Too late.

Without any warning, Darius and Emerus leap at each other, colliding in mid-air with their arms outstretched and their teeth bared. Each prince grips the other's arms, digging fingers into strong flesh as they fall back to the stone floor below.

Emerus is the first to strike, throwing an elbow into Darius' sternum that knocks him back a few steps. As he stumbles, Emerus follows up with a swift kick to the thigh, dropping his brother to the ground. When Emerus makes to kick again, Darius swiftly recovers and catches his brother's leg, twisting and violently forcing Emerus to jump and spin as the only way to keep the bone from breaking.

I'm watching every MMA fan's wet dream and hating every second of it.

Darius pounces on his brother, but Emerus catches him with his feet and throws him back with his strong thighs. The two both stand slowly, squaring off for another round. This time Darius goes on the offensive, feigning a punch and then catching his brother with a roundhouse kick to the shoulder. The blow throws Emerus off balance but doesn't bring him to the ground.

"Your legs seem weak, brother," Emerus says with a slight smile. "Not as forceful as when you were young."

Darius smiles back, and it's just so unbelievable to me that they're poking fun when one of them is about to die.

"I've been on the run for weeks," Darius says. "Fear not, I'll get my second wind."

Just as he finishes the word "wind," Darius propels himself like a torpedo, feet first and somehow spinning through the air. It's a move I've probably seen in a video game. You know, where physics don't matter.

His feet connect with Emerus' stomach, and while the younger brother tries to grab hold of the weaponized legs, there's too much torque. He falls back and Darius lands on top of him, pinning his arms to the ground with his knees. Emerus grimaces under the weight while trying to kick free, but Darius holds strong.

As Darius lifts his hands to his brother's throat, I

try to get inside his mind. I don't have anything to say, but I want to listen in. I need to know what could possibly be going through a person's head in a moment like this.

It's a confusing jumble inside Darius' mind, and I think I hear fragments of thoughts from Emerus as well. I'm sure the connection is strong between these siblings.

Ask for mercy, I hear Darius say. I can't make out a response, but it's clear from looking at him that Emerus doesn't plan to concede.

Darius digs his fingers into the skin around Emerus' neck, and the possibility of a gruesome murder becomes very apparent.

Please.

Darius asks again, but Emerus only kicks harder. Blood now drips from the younger brother's throat and the elder's grip tightens.

I honestly don't know if Darius has the heart to kill his brother, and the hesitation suggests he wouldn't do it, but I'm not willing to find out. I've found a better way. At least I think I have.

"Stand guard," I say to Zev and Rune, handing Rain to the fae. "I'm not sure how the vampires are going to react to this."

"React to what--"

"*Éget!*"

Before Zev can ask his question, my wand is up and shooting fire at Darius. Flames lick all around his naked back as he dives to the ground, trying to smother the blaze.

As soon as he's off his battered brother, I take aim and say "*menő,*" extinguishing the fire. Darius lies still as steam rises around him. He and Emerus sprawl out on the ground, both looking worse for wear.

What are you doing? Darius says in my mind, clearly still in agony from the burn.

Trying another way, I answer.

I walk forward, coming to a stop between the brothers, turning in a circle to look at all of the vampires. None of them makes a move toward me, but it feels like that could change in an instant. Zev and Rune quickly follow, standing at my sides in case some shit goes down.

"This won't save you," I say to the crowd. "Losing one of your leaders isn't how you gain a king. If Emerus got his goddamn head ripped off, would that make you swear allegiance to Darius?"

I was hoping for a more responsive crowd, maybe someone to throw out an Amen, but all I get is stone-faced silence. I guess I'll keep going.

"Darius' blood runs in my veins. Our minds and

bodies are bound, and I feel the reverence he has for this kingdom. But I've watched you tear each other apart, giving in to your bloodlust even as Vaemor crumbles and war wages on without an end in sight. You're so blinded by a tradition of violence that you've lost sight of the real enemy. It's not Darius. It's certainly not Emerus."

Emerus has slowly pushed himself up to one knee. He still looks pretty roughed up, but he's on the road to recovery. Darius is also sitting upright now and only a little bit of smoke billows off his burnt back. I'll have to remember to apologize for that later, and maybe send Rune to find some aloe. I take a breath and look back to the crowd, hoping to deliver a strong finale.

"Your enemy has never been the witches, it has never been the fae, it has never been the wolves. Until a few weeks ago, your only adversary was the prophecy. But now you have a real problem. Now there's a deranged man with a fleet of dragons and a massive army. He destroyed your city, killed your king, and he'll be back to take more of your lives if you don't do something about it."

No one speaks, so it's time to make the final pitch, and then my idea has run its course.

"We're going to stop him. If it's going to work, we

need your help. All of your help. Darius, and Emerus. If that means lighting you all on fire so you stop fighting each other, then that's what I'll do."

I raise my wand, now aimed at Emerus.

"So what's it gonna be?"

CHAPTER SEVEN

The tension is thick in the Pit as Emerus weighs his options, and I fake full confidence in my ability to follow through on my big speech.

I mean, I'll definitely unleash my wand powers on anyone who tries to kill me, Rain, or any of the guys. Whether we would survive the after-effects of that is less certain.

Still. I wait. Wand held high.

And if there's a trace of nerves making my hand shake, well… I try to ignore it and hope everyone else will too.

"You're playing with fire," Emerus says, his eyes narrowing at me.

My lips twitch and I can't help but channel a little AJ 'tude with this guy as I hold out a hand and let fire dance on my palm. "Haven't you heard? I *am* the fire."

Tread carefully, Darius says in my mind. *My brother is not one to trifle with.*

I'm not trifling, I say. *I'm trying to salvage our plan. A little help would be great.*

While I'd love to reach out to Zev and Rune to aid me, I know they aren't the most welcome in the vampire kingdom. It's up to me and Darius.

Not that I'm exactly welcomed with open arms, but they certainly have done their damnedest to get me here. They also just watched me light the traitorous brother on fire, so I'm not sure anyone's gunning for me yet.

"One of us will have to become king," Emerus says. "If we don't complete our duel…"

He's awfully cocky for a vamp who was about to face real deadness, I tell Darius. His lips twitch as he tries to suppress a laugh.

Emerus narrows his eyes, and though I feel a push in my mind--like he's trying to get inside my thoughts--I resist. The sexy brother glowers at me and I keep my face schooled in total innocence. Let him fester. I owe him nothing.

Darius stands and walks away from the center of the Pit, heading toward the woman carrying the crown. Everyone nearby shoots odious glares as he snatches the royal headwear, but no one tries to stop him.

"I have a simple solution," Darius says as he turns back to his brother, but Emerus cuts him off before he can get to the point.

"You can't just take the crown and expect our people to follow you after betraying our king." His voice catches, and once again I wonder at his relationship with his father. Were they close? Is he as evil as daddy vampire was? I don't get that vibe, but I can't get a read on this guy and Darius has never gushed about family. Though I try to dig deeper into my mind connection with Darius, to see if I can pull the answer up the way I learned to speak Hungarian, the effort is in vain.

I squint, a sudden throbbing headache puncturing my concentration.

Darius quickly glances my way, a grimace on his face, and I can tell he's feeling what I am. Knowing he must stay focused on the pressing issue, he shakes it off and he returns his attention to his brother.

"Our *king*," Darius says with a solid dose of disdain, "betrayed many when he waged war against everyone who wasn't a vampire. When he sent assassins after Bernie and Rain. When he let an unproven interpretation of an ancient prophecy destroy our kingdom. One of us will have to undo his many centuries of damage."

Darius maintains eye contact with his brother for a long time, and I resist the urge to try and listen in. It's clear there's a battle of the alphas going on internally and I don't want to get in the way.

Sometimes doing nothing, saying nothing, is the right course of action, albeit the much harder one to follow. I'm itching to make them talk, but I bite my tongue.

For a moment, the sheer insanity of all of this once again smacks me in the psyche. I should be tending bar and telling the regulars to go home to their wives, not playing chicken with the two royal princes of the vampire kingdom, but here we are.

The rest of the vampires might as well be mannequins, so still and quiet and oddly patient. Previous interactions had me thinking of this race as angsty and always on the go, but that might have something to do with them chasing and trying to abduct me. Now that we're all standing around and dealing with the future of their kingdom, I don't think any of them have so much as inhaled since this showdown between brothers began.

When the silence continues, I reject my commitment to staying out of it. Typical Bernie.

"Your numbers were decimated, and that is a tragedy" I say. "But your king was killed by an army of dragons and a guy who seems pretty eager to destroy you. We may not be natural allies, but we share a common enemy. Like it or not, you know we are stronger together. I'm not all that thrilled to be allying with kingdoms that have been trying to kill me and my baby, but sometimes you gotta make exceptions. So, are you going to be smart about this, or are you going to fight over your dad's hat while everyone dies?"

Darius walks over to Emerus, and I suck in my breath as we wait to see what he will do.

"I am the first to admit I have mixed loyalties," Darius says. "I am bound, by honor, by blood oath..." he glances at me, "and by choice, to Bernadette and her child. She has my heart, what is left of it."

His words soothe an ache that has been growing in my soul since his first perceived betrayal. Really since the moment he drank that potion and our entangled spirits were torn from one another.

"What are you saying, brother?" Emerus asks.

I'm encouraged by his use of the word brother instead of, say, traitor. Perhaps we're making progress.

Rather than answer, Darius steps forward, and I sense what he's about to do before he does it. Still, the act itself is emotionally moving. It feels heavy with meaning and future consequence.

Darius places the crown on his brother's head and then takes a knee, bowing. "I hereby relinquish my rightful place as the next king and bequeath this duty to my brother, Emerus of Vaemor."

The sound of murmuring vampires is not something easily described. Their voices carry on a different wave. Not quite words, not quite music, something in between but entirely new. Still, it's clear to all of us that what Darius has done is unprecedented.

Emerus, for his part, hasn't breathed since the crown was placed on his head.

Like he forgot to exhale.

I, however, still seem to need human amounts of oxygen, and so I suck in a breath and exhale as if I've just emerged from the depths of the ocean.

I'm pretty sure Rune and Zev use real air to breathe as well, but they're more inconspicuous than myself, which unfortunately results in me making an alarmingly human sound in an arena full of immortals.

All eyes turn to me, and despite being fundamentally opposed to blushing, I feel the blood rush to my cheeks.

"All hail King Emerus?" I say, my voice lacking in conviction as I try to navigate dicy vampire politics.

Color me shocked when a throng--I'm going with throng because they didn't cover vampire group names at Julliard--of vampires echo my words.

"All hail King Emerus."

Figuring it's best to err on the side of kissing ass right now, I bend the knee, mimicking Darius and hoping women don't have a whole different code of conduct.

Kneel! I say to Zev, who is stubbornly glaring at Emerus and refusing to budge.

Even my gentle fae is standing tall, his chin jutted out in uncharacteristic defiance.

Seems the other princes might be ready to form alliances but haven't reached the point of allegiances. Fair enough. When Emerus finally nods his head, tension eases from my shoulders. Darius stands, and I hear the two brothers exchange some thoughts I can't understand. Even though I can't translate, I have a strong sense they're speaking amicably.

In a show of good faith, I lower my wand.

Emerus raises his hand to draw everyone's attention to him, as if all eyes weren't already glued to the new king. Still, a little showmanship is probably a good quality in a leader. "Your proposal will be given due consideration," he says to me. "I will honor the codes of knighthood and guarantee your safety in our kingdom. Then I will give you my answer."

Consideration? That's all we get?

Hey, didn't you just make him king?? I ask Darius. *Wouldn't helping us out be the brotherly thing to do in response?*

I did make him king, yes, Darius responds. *And now he's going to decide what he feels is best for his kingdom.*

He says this like it's law, but it seems a little ridiculous.

Hot as my temper may be, I keep my freaking mouth shut as Darius stands and gestures for me to come forward. "Emerus, I'd like to officially introduce you to Bernadette Morgan. She's... very special."

Emerus nods his head in acknowledgment, so I follow his lead and hope I'm not embarrassing myself but also like, so what? It's really confusing being a woman in a normal world. It's extra extra confusing being a woman--a witch--and constantly bouncing between different cultures and worlds.

I follow Darius' and Emerus' lead as the two walk down from the Pit and head across a wind-swept patio of stone, orange dirt and cacti-like plants.

I can feel Zev's annoyance at this subservient treatment, but I admonish him to keep silent. A lot is riding on this partnership, and giving the new king 'tude won't do anything to help our cause.

We are ushered into a room that looks extravagant for one person but a bit cramped for four.

I don't need my mental/emotional connection to Darius to know that this was his room.

I try to take in every detail, gleaning as much as I can from my lover's life before we met. Frankly, there's not a lot to take away from it.

It's an austere space, with a large bed, a dresser, a desk and a fireplace with one chair set beside it. A door on the north wall leads to what I hope is some semblance of a modern bathroom, because my bladder has been stretched to capacity and I have to pee like I've never had to pee before.

A woman's postpartum bladder does not pause for war, it seems. This is another thing they didn't include in the What To Expect books. Honestly, they need a whole subseries on what to do when you have a baby and crazy paranormal shit happens.

I can't even pay attention as Emerus and Darius say their farewells. I'm legit trying not to pee myself.

When my kinda brother-in-law leaves, I instantly turn to Darius. "Tell me there is a bathroom?"

He points to the door I've been pinning all my hopes on and I don't even pretend decorum as I beeline it to relief.

What awaits me is less than encouraging.

There's a hole in the floor. That's it.

I eye it skeptically, but the urgency in my bladder propels me forward.

The pit is deep, and I can't smell or see what awaits anyone who might fall into it.

Though this does nothing to give me comfort, I stand over the hole and drop my pants, squatting and trying to aim as best I can.

What I wouldn't give for a shewee right now.

Last summer, AJ couldn't stop talking about a thing that could let us girls pee standing up like boys. At the time it seemed ridiculous and I told her so. Now, I'm eating my words as I try not to fall into the neverending pee pit. I'm also fighting back tears thinking of AJ. I need to get to her and Erzsébet ASAP to make sure everyone's okay.

I finish my business and try to shut my emotions down, knowing sadness won't get me any closer to finding my friend. Cleaning myself is a challenge best not discussed in polite company. When I return to the guys, I desperately wish for a proper bathroom, and I tell them so.

"This isn't...civil."

But honestly, we are all too exhausted to care.

The bed isn't big, but it's big enough. We arrange ourselves as best we can, with Darius on an edge, then me, Rain, Zev and Rune. It doesn't take long for us all to fall asleep.

I expected nightmares, but when I wake sometime later, it's a relief to realize I had a dreamless sleep after all the horror of the previous day.

I'm especially grateful to see a platter of food readied for those of us with human-esque stomachs. I feed and care for Rain then help myself to dried fruit and dried meat.

I'm surprised to wake before the guys, but am glad I've had a few moments to myself with my child before they rise.

I can feel the tension rolling off Darius as soon as he moves from the bed.

"My brother will make a decision shortly," he says.

I don't ask him how he knows. I assume it's either a vampire thing or a brother thing. Either way, time to get ready for what's to come.

Darius looks sallow and pale and when Rune takes Rain, I pull the vampire into the makeshift bathroom. "Feed on me."

He shakes his head, refusing. "I've betrayed you."

"Oh my lord, you are a pain in the ass. You need blood; I have blood. I'll get over the betrayal, but only if you stay... undead. And not like dead dead."

Frustrated by his unnecessary restraint, I pull him toward me and push his mouth towards my neck. It doesn't take much more than that to get him to feed.

I wish I could avoid the pleasure I feel in this act. I'm still processing the deceit, even though I understand the motivation. Nevertheless, I can't deny the relief present in the act of giving my life essence to him.

Zev and Rune have finished the refreshments by the time Darius finishes feeding, and I strap Rain to my chest as we make our way through winding halls to Darius' brother.

We find him sitting on a throne, with attendants on either side. He's wearing his father's crown and totally looks like he's practiced sitting on the throne before. I narrow my eyes at Emerus, suddenly suspicious of his motives as a wave of unease rides over me.

I want to flee.

To take my men and run.

And this urge makes me extra nervous.

Be careful, I say. *Something doesn't feel right.*

Darius doesn't reply. Instead, he focuses on his brother. "What have you decided?" he asks without preamble.

Emerus takes a long pause before speaking, making me doubt he's going to give a simple thumbs up to my request. He gestures to a couple plush pillows on the floor in front of his throne. "Please. Sit."

The hair on my neck stands on end at his words and I suck in my breath and hold my wand tightly in my hand, ready for whatever he's about to say. Darius sits without hesitation, so I steel my nerves and follow his lead.

"I have decided to offer an alliance to your cause and any who might join it, to stop Timót and his army. After that is done, I make no promises of peace."

"Understood," Darius says. He seems relieved by his brother's words, but I still feel like there's more to come. Emerus holds up a finger, proving me right when I had really hoped to be wrong.

"I have one condition to this agreement. It's not particularly pleasant, but it aligns with our laws... and it's non-negotiable."

Shit. This isn't good. I want to tell Darius to run. I want to blast Emerus with my wand before he has a chance to speak. Making him king was not the right call. Amiable as he may have been before, Vladimir's crown has made him shitty. I just know it.

"I will give the support of the vampires," Emerus says with a look of unearned triumph in his eyes, "if you, dear brother, agree to accept your due punishment."

Darius stiffens at my side and I shudder at whatever he is trying to avoid thinking. Whatever it is, it absolutely terrifies a vampire who almost never gets scared.

My heart feels on the precipice of breaking at the newly crowned king's next words. "I sentence you to the Tomb of Time for three passages of the moon. You will suffer one day for your sins, one day for mine, and one day for our fallen father, for whose death you will accept the blame."

Darius looks more like death than any vampire I've ever seen. His light skin is even lighter, his dark eyes sullen, his mouth slightly agape. Yet still he nods, accepting this fate I still don't understand.

What is the Tomb of Time? I ask, trying to hide the panic I feel. *What does this mean?*

Darius doesn't look at me or answer, toiling with too much panic of his own. Instead, I get a response from Emerus.

A chamber, deep in the bowels of our kingdom. Time passes at its own speed there. One day lasts for a thousand years.

His words hit me right in the knees, and if I wasn't already seated I would surely fall.

My sweet lover, who only just came back to me, will be locked away for three millenia.

CHAPTER EIGHT

My world spins and I feel dizzy, but I can't tell if it's me or Darius.

Most likely it's both of us.

I don't understand anything beyond the unfathomable number I just heard. *Three thousand years?* I'd be worked up if he'd said a week. This is unconscionable. I'd think it was a joke but the fear I feel in Darius makes it seem very real.

"No way. Hard pass."

Emerus frowns and Darius hisses in my mind. *Do not be foolish. We haven't been given a choice.*

What are you saying? We'll all be dead!

Darius gives me a sideways look, and it seems like I've missed something. He hesitates a moment before

I push him. *What don't I get about three thousand years in a tomb?*

He speaks to me slowly, like he's finding the silver lining in some really bad news. *Only three days will pass before I see you again. It will be but a short while for you, but I will live through three thousand years of solitude. It was a punishment designed specifically for the immortal.*

That clears things up, sort of. It makes me happy in one respect, because three days isn't so bad--for me. But to leave Darius here knowing what he's about to endure... I don't think I can do it. *No. Nope. Nada. Niet. Nine. I'm pretty sure those are all legit languages and all mean the same thing. No.*

Darius ignores me and addresses his brother. "May the sentence begin after my friends have left for the fae kingdom?"

I grab Darius' hand and squeeze it hard, digging my nails into his palms. "No. I do not agree to this at all, and I am not leaving without you."

"I'm not sure who you think is seeking your agreement," Emerus says with all the condescension of a king who earned his crown by lucking into the right bloodline. Kings suck.

"Listen, buddy," I start speaking well before I know what I'm going to say, but I'm sure I'll figure something out. "You're on that throne because I didn't let Darius kill you. You're alive because Timót doesn't want me dead."

"And you're alive because I helped you and your baby hide from the dragons," he answers, sneaking in a little fact that weakens my argument a hair. "We both have a debt to each other, which is why I'm willing to join forces with sworn enemies."

He looks at Zev and Rune for this last line, clearly less than pumped about having princes from the other kingdoms as guests. The fae and the werewolf stare back, less than thrilled about visiting the vampire city.

Emerus stands and walks over to me. At first, it feels like another power move and I grip my wand more tightly. Then he raises his hand in a classic "I come in peace" sort of way, and I try to quell my anger and my nerves. He stops a few feet from me, a thoughtful look on his face, trying to choose his words wisely.

"Outside these walls, the vampires are afraid, directionless, and angry. I intend to convince them this is a cause worth joining, but you cannot forget that a day ago, their previous king had your child on our sacred altar. Victory was declared, and then many of us died."

He turns his attention to Darius, and I sense a bit of remorse in my blood. The two brothers feel an equal sadness that it's come to this.

"I trust my brother," Emerus goes on. "I may be hurt by his priorities, but I understand them. And, as you both might be surprised to hear, I share many of Darius' feelings about our dead father."

Thank God. The jury's been out on Emerus this whole time, but the fact that he's not totally blind to his dad being horrible will make this united front thing a little easier.

"It pains me to bestow this punishment, but it must be done," King Emerus continues. "Darius knows as well as anyone that our people won't commit to me or a new way unless there's penance for the betrayal."

Darius doesn't have to speak or nod or anything for me to know he agrees. I still want to fight it, but it's clear I'm not going to have any authority on the matter.

"One day," I counter, putting my last bit of hope on a haggle. "One thousand years of tomb torture seems like plenty, right?"

The understanding look fades from Emerus' face, and he's instantly back to being a king with a boner for himself. "No. The sentence begins in one hour."

He heads back to his throne and a couple of vampire guards, who up until now had been creepily hidden in the shadows, move to escort us out. Darius turns to leave without any resistance, and I'm forced to follow.

We walk in silence back to Darius' cramped quarters, the guards on our heels to make sure we don't try anything funny. Once inside the small room, we stand for another few moments of quiet. Zev is the first to speak, and the softness in his voice shows he's plenty worried for his friend.

"We'll be waiting for you," he says. "In four days, we'll all be laughing about this. Or three thousand years and one day, for you."

Darius smiles, if only to acknowledge the werewolf's attempt at cutting the tension.

"You won't wait here," the vampire says. "You'll need to move on to the other kingdoms, to warn and persuade the others. It's possible Timót has already staged another attack."

"We also need to get to AJ and Erzsébet," Rune says. I feel a brutal mix of terror and excitement as I think about finding my friend, and worrying about whether or not she's okay. Rune takes my hand, helping me to manage the emotional overload.

For three days, I'll be torn apart, wondering

what's happening to Darius. For infinitely more time than that, he'll suffer in ways my human brain can't begin to comprehend.

But that's just the way it has to be.

When it's done, we'll all be alive, and that's the most I can hope for on any given day. Maybe we can find him a good undead therapist to help him process three thousand years of torture that only he experiences.

"Let's go," I say to Zev and Rune, though I keep my eyes on Darius. The last twenty-four hours have lasted a lifetime. I thought it might take longer for me to process and move past the deception that brought us here, but I don't need any more time. Darius acts almost exclusively out of love for me, and I'm surprised I couldn't see that the whole time.

Whatever claim to pain I might still have pales in comparison to what he's about to go through, and now all I feel is fear and sorrow for this man I love.

"We'll give you two a moment," Zev says. I let the werewolf take Rain from me, and my baby steps outside with two of her three paranormal dads. If we ever make it back to our world, she's gonna have the best Bring Your Parent To School days.

When the door shuts behind us, Darius and I are immediately in each other's arms, kissing fiercely.

God, I've missed him. And goddammit, I will miss him.

"How will you find us?" I ask, when we finally come up for air.

"I will always find you," he answers. "On any world, in any realm, I will find you."

The magical fusion of our souls might be weaker than it once was, but the bond of our love is as strong as ever. I trust him, and I know I'll see him soon. My heart will break for him every second we're apart, but then it will mend. And I hope he will mend from this as well.

I give him one last kiss, trying to inhale his spirit, to keep him inside me as we separate. I'll need his strength as we start this next leg of our journey.

And he'll need my strength even more.

Rune, Zev and I stand in quiet thought outside Darius' door. There's really not much to say. Again, Zev is the one to break the somber mood and push us forward.

"We've only got three days until Darius shows up and starts bragging about how much longer he's lived than the rest of us. Better get a move on."

It's a good enough line to make Rune smile, and I give the slightest grin. I'm not at all in a laughing mood, but I appreciate Zev's efforts.

"Let's go find AJ," I say, wiping my cheeks that had become damp without my knowing. "How do we get there, where is she, what's next?"

"This part of our realm hides behind the Kilarean Mountains," Rune says. "That's what keeps sunlight away, but it also means the land is narrow between the mountains and the sea. We'll start heading south, and trust your powers and intuition to guide us to Erzsébet and AJ."

I want to ask what intuition he's talking about, because I have yet to see an improvement in my sense of direction. I decide to leave my pride intact and save the self deprecation for when I actually get lost

"Lead the way," I say to my two Sexies.

With a quick look at the vampire guards who wait to escort Darius to the Tomb, we head down the hall and out into the open.

Vampires watch us go, and I'm banking on Emerus having told them they're not allowed to kill us. Trust is a crazy thing, as it can get you killed as easily as it can save you. If I didn't trust Emerus' word, I might start a fight and die. If I trust him and he's a liar, I'll get killed when I'm not looking. I clutch Rain a little tighter, offering my thumb as a pacifier while we walk.

Nearing the edge of the vampire city, it looks like

the trust was earned. Hundreds watch us leave, none of them make a move to harm us. That's one fear I can let go of; time to move on to the next.

Coming into this kingdom I was roped to a dragon, surrounded by evil strangers and emotionally destroyed on pretty much every level. On my way out, I can look around with a little less trepidation. I'll need to be alert and paying attention to whatever signs and landmarks might jar my memory and point me in the right direction.

Trouble is, this part of whatever world we're in has nothing but rocks and dust. It's like walking across the salt flats in the middle of the U.S., but somehow less appealing.

I look behind us at the city, trying to remember the direction from which we entered. Seems like the best bet is to walk straight into the nothingness and then reassess in a few hours.

We walk for a couple minutes before I feel eyes on me. Judgemental, questioning eyes.

"What?!" I snap at both Rune and Zev as I spin around to face them. "I feel your stares and I'm not vibing. What's up?"

Zev tries to hide a smile while Rune cocks an eyebrow, falling into their typical reactions to my sass.

"Is your plan really to retrace your steps through the barren stone land?" Rune asks.

"Even though you came in on a dragon, hundreds of feet above?" Zev tacks on.

"Right now, yeah, that's my plan," I say, equally annoyed with the attitude and my dumb ideas.

"You're a witch, love," Zev points out, like a sexy asshole. "You've got spells and powers... and you've got access to your memories that you've never had before."

Huh? Access to my memories? I cannot wait to know more about myself than everyone else seems to, because this shit is getting old.

"Step out of your mind," Rune says, sounding a little too much like a guru who's full of crap. "You get lost in your thoughts and can't see what's there."

This mumbo jumbo is going to drive me insane, but before I can tell them as much, Zev asks a final question.

"Where did you leave AJ?"

At the same time as the words *I don't know* flash through my head, so does an image of my dear friend, collapsed on the ground. I see her in my mind's eye, reliving the memory as it happened while I was there. Then, something shifts. I'm not looking through my eyes in the moment, but later as the dragon lifted into the air. I go higher and higher, AJ getting further away but still remaining in view.

It's the craziest thing. It's like I'm rewatching my flight to the vampire kingdom but from a different point of view. The DVD of my memory has special features and it's blowing my mind.

The vision dances through my head a few times, and I slowly piece together a direction and a general area. She's a few miles away, not nearly as far as I thought. When I pull myself out of my thoughts, both Rune and Zev are smiling.

"Did you learn anything?" Zev asks with a smirk.

I nod, still not fully believing what I saw. "How?"

"Magic opens the mind," Rune says, sounding like a stoner but still making a good point. "You aren't beholden to the linear thoughts of a human anymore. You have an extra eye."

Hell yeah I do.

I take one last peek into my past to get my bearings, then start to walk with a determined pace. "She's this way," I say with blooming confidence.

About ten steps in, the boys ruin my swagger.

"What? Why aren't you moving?"

"You've got a magical mind, love," Zev says as he steps towards me. "But you're not very fast."

He gives me a quick kiss and a bite of the lip,

then transforms into a wolf. I swallow a small amount of pride and climb onto his back. "That way," I say, pointing to the horizon.

Rune breaks into a sprint, and we all charge off, guided by my new, badass witch vision.

The land passes quickly beneath Zev's paws and Rune's feet. I'm sure Zev could outpace the fae if he wanted, but Rune runs plenty fast when compared to a non-magical sprinter, and I can tell we're getting closer to the mark.

Even though the landscape still looks the same, I sense we're nearing the portal and the spot where AJ fell. I squint, trying to make out anything I see in the distance. Hundreds of feet away, the faint outline of a shape catches my eye. It could be a rock, it could be nothing, but we're going that way.

A few of Zev's strides closer and I know we're in the right place. My skin crawls just nearing the spot I had to deal with so many blows--AJ, Darius, Timót... Andor. I haven't processed that one enough. Deceitful and criminal as the little man was, I took a life. As soon as my brain makes space for it, I'm sure that will haunt me.

The shape I saw in the distance has now become a human form, and my heart skips far too many beats as I try to figure out who it is. A few feet closer I spot the flowing gown, the long red hair, and the general poise of a powerful witch.

Erzsébet.

Standing.

Over AJ.

It's been a day, maybe more, maybe less, and my best friend, my non-amorous life partner, my sister from another mister, still lies right where we left her.

The wound from Darius' betrayal opens back up a tiny bit.

My desire to shoot Timót out of a canon and into the sun returns with a vengeance.

When we're probably twenty feet away, with Zev still running at a good clip, I find myself standing and leaping off his back, using our momentum to propel me forward. In my mind, I look incredible, flying toward the ground in slow motion. In reality, there's a good chance I'm about to break my ankles.

Maybe it's the sight of Erzsébet that has my brain remembering tricks from my training, or maybe it's the lesson I just got on how to access my mind--I point my wand at the ground I'm sailing toward and say "*párna*." When my feet touch the stone they sink in gently, and I stick the landing like a professional, magical gymnast.

It probably saved me half a second, but I look freaking awesome.

"What's wrong?" I ask Erzsébet, saving our pleasantries for later when I know what's up with my fallen friend.

The witch queen looks at me, then at my feet as she admires my abilities, then back to my face with concern.

"She's alive, insomuch as she has a pulse," she says. "But I must know the spell in order to summon an antidote, if any exists."

For a split second, I revert back to the idiot brain I was trained to use by other idiots and family members who lied to me about my powers (no hard feelings, Tilly, I love you forever). Then I remember that I've got magic memories and I step inside my own mind, seeking out that moment that shot a harpoon through my heart, but now with the intention of undoing what was done.

"*Lélel nak a szikla*," I say with more certainty than I've ever said anything. From the outside looking in, I can see it all unfold clear as day. I can hear the spell as though my father were standing next to me, whispering it into my ear.

It sends a chill down my spine.

Erzsébet wears a dubious look. "Are you sure?"

I nod, now trusting my memories implicitly since I can watch them like a detective analyzing a surveillance video.

Erzsébet kneels by AJ again, studying her and listening for either breath or a heartbeat. "Bernadette," she says softly. "I need you to come put a hand on AJ's shoulder. Hold her steady while I cast a spell."

I'm eager to do anything and everything to help, but am consumed with guilt after leaving her alone. If I can't save her now, it's my fault. I'm a shit friend. I had no choice, AJ would have told me to go if she'd been able, but that doesn't change how I feel.

I follow the queen's instructions and kneel beside AJ's body, stiff as a board but still warm.

"I make no promises," Erzsébet says. "I've one trick to try, then this is in the hands of the Fates."

I place my hand on AJ's shoulder while looking into her frozen face. Even if she's alive, her face doesn't make it seem that way. It's almost too much to bear.

I squeeze her arm, sending as much of my life force into her through my fingertips as I can manage. I don't know exactly what Erzsébet expects of me, but I'm doing my best.

"*Élettel teli*," the queen says, a faint flicker of light

coming from the end of her wand. There's no fanfare, nothing that makes me or Zev or Rune jump back in surprise. Only a slow breeze that circles around and wafts into AJ's slightly open mouth.

The lack of excitement makes me fear the worst. If the spell had worked, AJ would have shot up instantly, wondering where she was, looking for a vampire to fight.

I'm starting to crumble. I don't know if I can do any of the things I need to do with this hanging over me.

I lean over her, tears starting to trickle down my nose. She's still completely rigid, her hands balled into tight fists. I stare into her eyes, wondering if I'm about to say goodbye.

And then she blinks.

Her chest starts to rise and fall and her eyes wander around, trying to figure out where she is.

Finally, her gaze settles on me.

"You bitch."

CHAPTER NINE

I completely dissolve. I throw myself on top of AJ and start to cry like a baby, nearly crushing my actual baby between us.

For the first time in our long and storied friendship, AJ's crying as hard as I am.

"I watched you leave," she sobs. "I was paralyzed, and I watched that asshat tie you up and then you all flew off on dragons. Jesus Christ, B, I've never been so sad."

I help AJ up so we're both sitting. She takes a break from crying and talking to lean over and kiss Rain. I notice she's got a pendant clutched tightly in her hand, something I don't remember ever seeing before.

"Not many can withstand being turned to stone," Erzsébet says.

"Is that what happened to me?" AJ asks.

"More or less. Your body stops moving, even your cells and blood. Seems you have an impressive constitution."

AJ stares down at her pendant, then back up at me. I've got questions, but they can wait.

We resume crying for a few more moments, then AJ looks around to take stock of our present company.

"Witch lady, wolfy, elf man... where's the bloodsucker?"

When I open my mouth to answer, the lump in my throat gets too big for words to come out. I try to feel for our connection, to see if I can sense where he is or what he's going through, but there's nothing. Not a trace of Darius. He's in the Tomb.

I should have answered AJ's question more quickly, because now she's in a panic.

"No. He can't be dead. He--"

"He's not," I say. "He's alive, but... it's complicated. Like really complicated, there's a whole time and physics thing going on that I don't understand. I'll explain it while we travel."

AJ looks at me with hope in her eyes but fear on her otherwise grimacing face.

"Are we going... home?"

I shake my head.

"Back to Budapest?"

I shake my head again.

"Land of the water nymphs?"

A final head shake breaks her spirits. "Goddammit, just tell me then."

I stand, then help her to her feet. AJ's always been the picture of exuberance, so when her knees give out and she hits the ground again, I'm more than slightly concerned.

"What's wrong? Are you hurt?"

She looks more confused than agonized. "Just so. Damn. Thirsty."

Before I can ask, Rune is kneeling by her side with a leather bladder. She practically breaks his thumbs as she takes it and drinks it all down in a couple gulps.

"Better?" Rune asks, turning the bladder upside down and shaking it to prove she finished every drop.

AJ licks her lips and then shakes her head. "No. I'm still wicked thirsty. Water nymph needs water."

She's being tongue in cheek about the whole

thing, but I get the feeling she's right. Rune's nod makes me even more sure.

"You need to do more than hydrate," he says. "I wonder if it's the water in your body that's kept you alive all these hours, and now it's nearly run out."

I look to Erzsébet to see if Rune's theory gets approved by the ancient witch. She nods as well. Seems like everyone agrees, which is awesome, but maybe we should do something about it?

"Where do we go for water?" I ask. "This clearly isn't the spot, so where do we go and how do we get there?"

Erzsébet adjusts her robes. "We can't find the help she needs in Vaemor. The vampire kingdom is toxic, as you might have noticed. We need to get to Aeve-lairith. The fae waters are renowned for their healing properties."

"She speaks the truth," Rune says with more than a little pride in his voice. "There is nothing more healing than water, and no water more healing than that of the fae. They say the ancient trees gained their spirits because of the waters that feed their roots. All of nature is more alive that is fed from these waters."

"Well, great, that's where we were going anyway, so maybe let's stop talking about it and get there," I say.

My own statement brings me to a very obvious question.

How the hell do we get to Aevelairith?

There has to be a portal here, because this is where I landed after Timót pulled me through the door underneath the Grand Hall. Looking around, I see nothing but barren grounds that stretch on indefinitely.

"You won't see the portal door, Bernadette."

Erzsébet's been doing a little mind reading these last few seconds, but her smile says she's got an answer that won't make me angry.

"The doorways between realms were opened shortly after the creation of all things, but the wars made them more of a danger than a useful means of conveyance. Aside from the singular room in our Budapest fortress, all the access portals have been hidden."

Cool. But also not.

"So how do we find our way out?"

Erzsébet turns her attention toward the ground, looking like an old woman who dropped a hairpin. "You just have to know where to look."

After staring at the ground for a minute or two, she pops up. "Here it is!"

We all move over, Zev and Rune each propping up AJ, to see what the powerful witch has found.

It's a rock.

Like, a pebble.

So... maybe she's lost it?

"*Felfed portál*," she says with her wand pointed at the tiny stone. In an instant, an undulating doorway sprouts up from the ground, standing in front of us like a vertical sheet of water.

"Shit," AJ says, vocalizing what I was certainly thinking.

"How the hell did you know it was that rock?" I ask, probably sounding more annoyed than I really am. Except, for real, how?

"I just... remembered. Come along, just a few seconds before it disappears."

And with that, she steps through the magical passageway and vanishes into another realm.

She remembered.

Of course. And if I ever end up back here, I'll remember as well. Though if I ever end up back here, I might just lay down and hope to die. This place sucks.

Zev and Rune edge through the portal, still supporting AJ and moving quickly and safely.

I step in after them, a million things running

through my head. I'm blissed the hell out to be back with AJ. I'm stoked to be in the company of another, more powerful witch. I need to feed and change my baby, and she's probably due for some tummy time.

I miss Darius beyond words. I miss his touch, I miss our connection, and I can't handle thinking about what he's experiencing.

And I'm glad we're on the move. Time to find some fae water and then go save the effing universe.

Round two of falling through the witches' portal doesn't mess me up nearly as much as the first time.

For starters, I'm not pushed through by a creepy little shit disguised as Rune. This magical journey between realms also doesn't involve my father, and though my heart aches constantly for the pain Darius is enduring, I'm at least not worried that my friends and lovers are being slaughtered by vampires. All of those things make this teleportative outing much less stressful.

When we pass through the crazy rock door in Vaemor, we end up right where I started, underground in Budapest. I have a brief longing to run up and feel sunshine, maybe eat a bagel, do some quick human things, but I know there's no time. Erzsébet shows us right to another point on the portal room star, this one directing to a doorway that will drop us somewhere in Aevelairith.

That's what *really* separates this trip from the first portal voyage.

Landing in a remote corner of the vampire kingdom, where the sun is permanently blocked by imposing mountains and a gray haze--that's pretty upsetting to the senses.

Conversely, when you pop out in a cave behind a waterfall, then walk through the cascading stream and your eyes fall on a green, luscious valley, with even more waterfalls in the surrounding hills and all manner of plant and animal life frolicking about, it's pretty awesome.

They keep telling me these kingdoms are part of the same world or realm, but I don't see how that could be. The vampires live on Mars or Venus, some arid rock with nothing that can sustain biological life. The fae live in the freaking Garden of Eden. Traveling from the Sahara to the Amazon wouldn't produce this stark a contrast.

"Portals aren't what I expected," AJ says as we stand on the face of a cliff that's overgrown with beautiful ferns and flowers. The clearest, most brilliant water I've ever seen splashes down behind us, pools at our feet and then falls again into the watering hole below. We're up high enough to see for miles.

Erzsébet flashes a skeptical grin. "What were you expecting?"

AJ shrugs, but the effort appears to exhaust her and she leans against Rune for support in her weakened state, clutching the pendant at her chest. "I don't know. Something crazy like a unicorn piss portal or something."

I burst out laughing. "Unicorn piss? That's absurd! And gross." I shudder imagining having to walk through Michael's pee stream in order to fast travel.

"Maybe," she says. "But it would be interesting."

"Interesting isn't always better, A."

She rolls her eyes at me. "Interesting is always better."

Everyone else seems to have tuned out of our convo, and for good reason. I'm certainly done with these unsanitary visualizations. I clutch Rain against my chest as I refocus on the breathtaking beauty around us. I just wish Darius were here to enjoy it with us. Albeit at night, where he won't get fried by the sun, which honestly feels glorious on my skin. I can't remember the last time I was out during the daylight hours. My poor child probably has a massive Vitamin D deficiency.

"Do you know where we are?" Erzsébet asks Rune, who's surveying the grounds with a twinkle in his eye.

"It's the Valley of Hilinea," the fae answers. "I visited here with my grandmother in my youth, to see the dance of the willows."

Erzsébet nods, and it's clear she wasn't asking for directions but rather checking to make sure Rune knew his history. With how powerful and spry the queen is, I sometimes forget that she's crazy old and sometimes just wants to talk about old stuff.

"Hilinea was a powerful, kind woman. I met her when I was a child, she would come give lessons to young witches learning to make potions. A pity that this valley took on her name after it was forcibly annexed from the witching realm. I don't imagine she would have approved."

It's a passive-aggressive dig, but years of persecution have earned her the right. Rune has nothing to say in defense, just a solemn nod of acknowledgement.

Everyone stands in silence for a moment longer, then the quiet breaks as AJ cannonballs into the water below, nearly giving me a heart attack.

"AJ!" I scream, worried when she doesn't resurface

immediately. Rune takes my hand, steadying my frayed nerves. "Wait. Watch."

So I do. I wait. I watch. I hope to heavens I'm not waiting and watching my best friend drown after being basically turned to stone.

I study the surface of the water looking for any signs of life, and if not for the calming effects of Rune, I'm sure I would be losing my mind right now.

I'm expecting her little head to bob up at any moment sucking in a huge breath, but then I remember she can breathe underwater and I feel like a huge idiot. Still, she's so weak that I'm not totally convinced all is well.

When something shoots out of the water and into the air like a playful dolphin, I nearly fall off the cliff. Rune catches me as I stare in awe.

AJ is flipping through the air laughing and hooting, and I don't blame her for one single second.

Her long blond hair dances in the wind, but now has streaks of teal blue through it. Her skin is iridescent and shimmers under the sun, and her legs... well, her legs are now fused into a beautiful teal fish tail that matches her eyes and the new streaks in her hair.

Also, she seems to have lost her clothes underwater, as she is totally naked now, save her jewelry and her newly acquired scales.

"AJ is... a mermaid?" I ask in awe.

"We always knew she was a water nymph," Rune says with a smile. "If the blood line is strong enough, they can take on a form similar to mermaids, though it's very rare. Their scales are different, and their gills are slightly larger."

"Right, so like the difference between a crocodile and an alligator."

Rune shrugs. "I suppose."

I grin. "AJ's gonna be thrilled to hear this is super rare. But why is it happening now and not all the other times she went into water?"

He looks at AJ thoughtfully. "A combination of things. It's the magical waters of these lands unlocking her deepest truth, and likely healing a fracture within that was keeping her separate from her magic. It's also that she knows who she is now," he says with a grin. "At any rate, she has the right idea."

Without warning, Rune plunges into the water below, joining AJ. He swims to the surface, shedding his wet shirt and climbing up on the water's edge. We've all got a million worries on our minds, but Rune is taking a break to feel at home. Water drips off his slender frame as he tilts his head back, eyes closed, feeling the warm sun on his face.

Zev quickly follows suit, swan diving into the water below and then joining the fae on the shore. AJ continues to dance with the water. I can't describe it in any other way. What she's doing right now is so much more than swimming, and I feel a twinge of envy at how connected she is with this element. It suits her.

I've got Rain strapped to my chest, and I'm not really one for high-diving, so I look to Erzsébet to see what she's got planned for her descent. My look is met with a sly smile.

"Hand me Rain and swim with your men and your friend," she says. "If I were an eon or two younger, that's what I would do."

It's a sweet offer, and a salient point. Who knows how many chances I'll have to dive from fae waterfalls into fae pools and then snuggle up with my werewolf mate? Plus I definitely want a closer look at AJ's tail.

I hand Rain and her harness to Erzsébet, panic for a second, then take the plunge. The fall is exhilarating and my heart is pounding hard in my chest when I hit the frigid water, but my body adapts quickly and it becomes a pure source of refreshment and magical regeneration.

AJ splashes up to me, using her tail to send a spray of sparkling water raining over me like a waterfall. "B! Look! I have a tail!"

I laugh as I tread water, weighed down by too many clothes. "I noticed. What's it like?"

She giggles and does a backflip, then resurfaces and sprays water from her mouth like a fountain. I just try not to think of the fish poop that's definitely in that mouthful. "It feels freaking amazing!" she says. "Like I was born to this. I never want to leave."

That innocent sentiment sends my heart lurching. In all our talks of me leaving Rowley, it never occured to me she might be the one to leave. Why would she want to go back to a town with such bad memories, where she's not treated great, when she could spend her life lazing in the sun and swimming like a fish?

Given the choice, I know which I would pick, and if it comes to that, I'll be happy for her.

Sensing my mood as always, she sprays me with water again, this time more forcefully. "Stop moping. I'm not leaving you, not even for a water paradise."

I smile and the words give me temporary comfort, but I hadn't realized until now that she could have a much more enjoyable life in this world. Is it possible to relocate? To become a permanent citizen of Aevelairith? Are there, like, immigration laws or paperwork to fill out? It's something to look into. I want my friend to live her best possible life, even if that isn't with me.

I swim to the shore with the guys and undress down to my underwear and bra. This gets me a few appreciative glances which I smile at before diving back in. I can understand why AJ never wants to leave. It's like swimming in the original waters of creation. I feel a bubbling of joy within me that radiates through my skin as it glows in the water. Everything feels possible, and suddenly the task of convincing a couple more rival kingdoms to align doesn't seem nearly as daunting.

Let's just hope no one from our worlds gets their hands on this magical treasure. It would be bottled up and sold on Amazon within a month.

I swim back over to AJ, who let's me more closely examine her skin and scales. "You're beautiful," I say in awe.

She smiles even wider. "This is the best thing to ever happen to me in my whole life, and it's all because of you," she says, growing suddenly serious, her eyes glossy with emotion. "Thank you, Bernie. You're my best friend in the world, and you've brought so much magic into my life, I can't even begin to tell you how you've changed me."

"I almost got you killed," I say, the words sticking in my throat painfully.

She rolls her eyes. "Please. First, I'm totally better. Better than better. I'm the best I've ever been. And your dipshit dad was responsible for that, not you. By that token, I almost got you killed when my ex showed up with a shotgun."

Solid point. In all the craziness, I'd nearly forgotten about that. Crazy how a guy almost killing you then dying by vampire-werewolf attack in your living room can seem so inconsequential in the right--or wrong--context.

"How about we chalk up our near death experiences to the asshole men in our lives and enjoy the awesomeness of this world. Cuz I am here for this."

I smile and nod my head. "Fair enough. Race you to the shore?"

What an idiot I am.

As kids I always beat her in pretty much every foot race.

But that wasn't in the water, and she wasn't sporting a mermaid tail.

She's laughing at me as she does a magnificent spiral in the air and lands near the shore in a blink.

I take a bit longer and am laughing along with her when I arrive.

She continues playing in the water, and I wave to Rain and Erzsébet, but realize they're no longer there.

A quick look around finds them having located an easier trail down, and now lounging under a weeping willow on a patch of thick green grass that looks like luxurious carpet. Erzsébet is giving Rain a bath in the magic waters, and my daughter's skin is glowing like mine as she babbles. I mouth a thank you to the witch and crawl out of the water to lay on the grass between Zev and Rune as they look up at the clouds.

Zev puts his arm around me and pulls me into his chest. His heat dries my undergarments quickly and the sun feels amazing on my skin. I close my eyes and soak in the rays, the calm, the bliss of this moment.

The water laps at our feet, pushed by the currents from the waterfall, and continues to work its magic on all of us.

I peak through eyelashes to see that Rain is now napping on the grass, Erzsébet keeping a close eye on her. AJ is lounging on a boulder pushing out of the water, like the Little Mermaid. Rune looks like he's napping, and Zev has his gaze locked on me.

"You're beautiful," he whispers, his lips now inches from mine.

"It's my waterfall look. Carefully cultivated," I

joke, tugging on the wet, wavy mess that is my hair now.

"It's a good look," he says with a grin. "The only flaw I can find in it is that you are wearing too much clothing."

I laugh. "Some would say I'm not wearing enough, given we're not alone."

"Who says being alone is a requirement for anything?" he asks, a darkly seductive look on his face.

"You're naughty. And I'm not having sex in front of everyone." Honestly, Rain is too young to know what's going on. I'm sure plenty of new parents have sex with their sleeping infant in a crib nearby. And AJ--Eh. Not really into exhibitionism, but we've seen worse from each other. Rune? Actually, the idea gives me a little tingle. But there is no way in hell or hades I'm getting frisky with the queen of witches eyeing us. Nope. Hard and fast and solid nope.

Zev sighs dramatically, then pulls me up with him in one smooth move and dives into the water with me.

With my skin freshly warmed by werewolf heat and the sun, the water is shockingly cold once again, but I relish it and duck my head to submerge myself completely. Zev joins me, and the water is so crystal clear we can see each other in detail.

He makes funny faces and reaches for me, and I try not to laugh and inhale the wrong oxygen source for my body.

My best friend may be easily able to switch between water and air with ease, but I'm still solidly in the air camp.

When he presses his lips to mine, the air from his lungs enters me, and I inhale him and kiss him, our bodies slipping against each other in an extremely pleasant way.

I wrap my legs around his waist and let the hardness of him press into me as he moans in my mouth.

He clearly has a larger storage of oxygen than me, but eventually we both run out of air and have to resurface.

I'm laughing and spitting water, so it takes me a moment to catch that the energy around us has changed.

I look to the shore and see Rune standing with his hands up. AJ is on shore, human legs returned, completely naked, also raising her hands.

And surrounding the shore are dozens of fae holding longbows, all of which are pulled tight and aimed straight at us.

Frantic, I look around to find Erzsébet and Rain, but they are nowhere to be seen. I say a silent prayer of hope that she left before being noticed and is taking care of my baby. Because whatever is going down right now isn't good, and I don't want my child anywhere near it. If Rain got away with the queen of the witches, I know she'll be safe.

The leader of the armed fae, a tall man with long black hair streaked with silver, steps forward. "Quite a lot of foreigners to be swimming in a sacred fae pool. Keep your wands where we can see them. Reach for a weapon or shift and you'll be dead."

I eye my wand on the shore and curse myself for not keeping it with me.

Zev and I approach cautiously, trying our best to stay out of view.

"Come out of the water, you two."

Not out of view enough, it would seem. We step onto dry land and move over to join Rune.

My usually calm companion glares at the man in charge with a hatred I have never seen on his face, even when confronting our most dangerous enemies.

"Hello cousin," Rune says. "I expected a warmer welcome than this."

His cousin smirks. "You weren't expecting a welcome at all, or else you wouldn't be sneaking in through the south end of the valley. Too bad for you we still run patrols to keep vampires and wolves out. Tell me, Rune, when did you become such traitorous trash?"

He grabs Rune by the neck and pushes him forward. The other fae take the rest of us by the arms and start marching us away from the water.

Before I can be corralled, I sprint over to grab my wand, but just as my fingers touch it a large boot comes down on my hand. I yelp in pain and feel a strong grip on the back of my head, pulling me up by my hair.

"No, no, no," Rune's cousin says. "You've caused enough trouble as it is. You can have your stick back when you're released from prison… should such a day ever arrive."

CHAPTER TEN

Where's *Rain?* I ask Zev mentally as we are pushed into a thick forest, the threat of being shot by an arrow ever-present.

They got away before they were seen. Don't worry, Erzsébet will protect Rain and find us later. His voice is husky in my mind, and there's a simmering rage he's barely repressing under his words. I glance at him and see his muscles bulging as he resists the urge to wolf out.

How do you know? I ask.

Because she's the queen of the witches, caring for the Last Witch, he says curtly. *What else would she do?*

It's the answer I hoped for, but I still breathe a deep sigh of relief at hearing it. As much as it terrifies me to have Rain out of my sight, there's no one I'd rather she be with, and I'm extremely happy they snuck off unseen.

I'm pulled out of my thoughts when I feel a guard's hand grab my arm and yank me forward. "Keep the pace," he says, his hard gray eyes boring into me. "So you're the witch everyone's been talking about? What's so special about you?" he hisses as he drags me along, his grip creating an instant bruise around my arm.

"Give me back my wand and find out for yourself," I spit back.

He squeezes even tighter, causing me to flinch. I really got the wrong impression about the fae; basing them all off Rune's pleasant demeanor was a big mistake.

The guard's eyes shift from me when we hear a low growl coming from my side. Zev easily rips out of the grasp of the surprised fae holding onto him and pushes my guard away from me, grabbing him by the throat in the process. "I will cut off any body part of yours that touches her again. Do you understand?"

Everyone stops walking to turn and look at us.

And AJ uses this moment to speak up. "Hey, I'm naked here in case you hadn't noticed!"

She. Looks. Pissed.

I have never seen my bestie this angry, and I've

seen her plenty riled up. I notice a few of the fae soldiers leering at her, and that makes my blood boil.

"You'll have to make due," Rune's dick bag cousin says as he turns away. "Keep moving, we don't have time for distractions. And you," he says to Zev. "Another move and I'll put an arrow through your heart, then turn you into a wolf-skin rug."

They push us along, no intention of heeding AJ's request. I'd love at least a shirt to cover a little skin, but poor AJ's naked as the day she was born.

"Ouch!" The fae holding onto AJ yelps and jumps back from her. We all stop and stare.

I widen my eyes at her hair, which is now floating above her head in the shape of spikes. That bitch used her water powers to make frozen daggers with her wet hair, and her captor now has a gash across his face that's seeping blood.

On the one hand, go girl. On the other, Rune's cousin hasn't been stingy with the threats. I'm not sure how far we can push before someone gets hurt.

AJ's eyes blaze, and the pendant she's clutching almost glows. "Give me and Bernie some clothes, or you won't like how this ends."

Rune's cousin sneers for a moment, then nods at two of his men. Looks like we walked up to the line but didn't cross it.

The guards take off their vests and hand them to us. AJ and I slip them on, and I feel a little more confident now that I'm a bit more clothed. The vest acts as a very sleeveless dress.

My guard does not touch me the rest of the hike, and he flinches every time Zev glances at him.

In fact, none of the guards get heavy-handed with us again, and I wonder if they realize we could for sure take them in a fight. Or if they have another reason for getting us to the royal family unscathed. I mean, Rune is their prince. That must account for something, right?

It's unfortunate we're surrounded by fae assholes, otherwise I'd really enjoy the scenery. As we get closer to the outer walls of Aevelairith, I notice more houses built within the trunks and branches of trees. We cross beautiful streams every hundred feet or so, walking over carefully carved wooden bridges.

We finally come to a giant drawbridge nestled between two mountain ridges. A handful of guards stand in front of the massive gate, while others lean out of turrets above, their bows drawn.

Rune's shitty cousin yells up to a guard stationed atop the barricade. "Lower the gate and send a runner to the palace. Tell the king and queen their son's come home."

The sound of gears turning echoes off the mountains as the drawbridge lowers. I sort of expect to see paved streets and something representing a city on the other side, but all I see are trees. As we start to move through the threshold and I can look higher, I see the city I wanted is mostly there, just several stories higher.

Bridges, branches, vines and ropes connect a massive overhead metropolis, held in place by every kind of tree you can imagine. Redwoods act as huge pillars for the bigger structures; birch trees grow in tight clusters to form barriers; incredible oaks reach in every direction, creating walkways on different levels. It's what a child might imagine a squirrel motel would look like, but full of grown adults and way more extravagant.

We're ushered along by our unfriendly captors. As we pass other fae, they seem intrigued and confused by us. Some of them recognize Rune and gasp. All in all, they strike me as more fae-like than the patrolling squad that found us.

Crap cousin reaches a massive sequoia trunk with a small opening and gestures for us to enter. The gesture isn't a suggestion, because our accompanying guards shove us ahead and don't give us a choice.

Inside the tree, a spiral staircase is carved along

the inner edge of the trunk. I can't explain how big this sequoia is, except to say I immediately forget it's a tree once we're in the trunk.

The stairs go up for quite a few flights, occasionally passing openings to branches that lead off to another tree. I start to wonder how long it took to build this place, then stop myself before a migraine sets in.

Finally we're shown an exit, though the doorway out of the tree doesn't really take us outside. Instead we find ourselves in a spacious chamber with a roof that looks to be made of enormous leaves. The walls are made from a variety of woods that seem fused together, creating a natural, rustic look.

At the end of the hall are three chairs, or humble thrones. The king sits in the center seat, his long white hair matched by a long, silky beard. Aside from being completely gray, he doesn't look that old.

The queen sits beside him, with curly hair I want to describe as blond, but it's just so damn light I can't tell. Maybe she's gone gray too, but it looks sort of like Rune got his coloring from her.

And on the other side of the king sits who I'm guessing is the princess, Rune's older sister. She somehow popped out of her mother with auburn hair, so I'm guessing that's how Rune's pop's was colored many moons ago.

Each of the three wears the same concerned expression, and they've all got their eyes on Rune.

We're led into the center of the room while more guards pour in and stand around the perimeter. You'd think the envoy accompanying the prince of this realm, all of whom just got caught skinny dipping and are still underdressed, would draw less hostile attention.

The king looks at each of us, then finally speaks. "Where are you coming from?"

"Found them at the Mystelian Falls," the cousin answers. "Marched them straight here."

The looks of concern on the royals' faces take on a shade of confusion.

"Did you not give them a chance to dress?" the queen asks.

"Well, your majesty, the intrusion--"

"As you can see by my borrowed vest that barely covers my ass and has to be pulled shut so you can't see my hoo-ha, no they did not."

Sometimes I wonder what movie AJ saw as a child that made her think speaking her mind at all times, no matter the company, was the best choice. The king and queen seem a bit taken aback, but then turn back to the leader of the guards.

"Why would you treat your cousin this way, Eliar?" Now the king looks upset, but not at us.

"My lord, he's betrayed you in more ways--"

"So you march him naked through the woods? If he's to be tried and put to death, so be it, but he is still your prince until that verdict comes, and I daresay I'm not going to give it."

The cousin, Eliar, chomps down on his lip so he won't dig this hole any further. The king rises and walks toward Rune, who kneels before his father.

"Stand, child," the king says, and as he does so the queen walks down to join them. "I don't need your forgiveness when I don't yet know what's happened. Above all, I'm overcome with gratitude to see you alive."

"Thank the gods," his mother said. "We've missed you, Rune."

On the heels of meeting Darius' father, and then thinking about my recent parental interactions, it feels like Rune hit the mom-and-dad jackpot. The sister also stands, looking happy to see her brother but staying a few feet back. While Rune embraces his parents, his sister does a quick survey of the rest of us. I'd probably do the same if I were in her shoes. She and I hold brief eye contact, but her stare lingers on Zev the longest.

Rune makes quick work of explaining what's happened. Since the king and queen--who I gather from the conversation are named Rivelis and Scocha, respectively--are good listeners with concern for their family, he's able to make salient points and gets them nodding pretty earnestly while describing the flawed view of the prophecy.

When he gets to the part about an alliance, the air gets sucked out of the room. Rune's sister, Revia, steps forward to join the conversation, her mood seeming very tense.

"What word do you have that they might hold their end of the bargain?" she asks. "And why would we ever trust that?"

I see the body language of the guards shift while the conversation turns to teaming up with the vampires. Centuries of battle and fending them off has made for some pretty bad blood, so to speak.

"We have word from their new king, and we have a sworn oath with the king's brother, Darius," Rune says.

Rivelis cocks an eye at Darius' name. "Your old friend? That vampire prince, you have an oath with him?"

Rune nods, and I really can't tell how his dad is reacting to this information. He slowly strokes his beard while digging through his memory.

"We liked him before this all started, I remember. Before he took on his father's disposition."

"Which has gone since he met Bernadette," Rune says, gesturing to me, "and her daughter."

Rivelis shows a warm smile as he walks over to me, but stops short.

"I can't believe I didn't ask... where is the Last Witch?"

Great question, sir. Where is the witch who has my baby? I'm about to ask that very question, when Rune comes in with an answer.

"The child remains in the Earthly realm with Erzsébet," he says. "Bernadette was pulled from that world without her baby, and as trying as that's been, it's kept the child safe."

It's a calculated lie, but I'm not quite sure why he's telling it. The king and queen seem to be entirely on his side. Now we're locked into not asking about-- or looking for--my baby and our very powerful companion.

Far be it from me to question Rune's assessment of the situation, especially in his own kingdom. As I move through these thoughts, my eyes again meet with Rune's sister's, and I can't quite get a read on what she's thinking. She looks away after a beat, and the king's voice draws everyone's attention.

"I, for one, am moved by your story and compelled to act," Rivelis says. "But not until I've spoken with the queen and spent some time in the Elder Roots. The issue of an alliance with the vampires comes with great delicacy."

"Unless we establish ourselves as the leading race with full authority," Revia says, "I see no case for such a coalition. It's a setup for betrayal."

"I agree... or rather, I would have,' Rivelis says, putting a hand on his daughter's shoulder, "but the death of King Vladimir and this argument against the prophecy turns my mind. After all, who among us doesn't want to see the end of this endless war?"

The king gestures to the whole room, bringing the dozens of guards into the conversation. A few give small nods, most stay stoically still. Revia doesn't look convinced, but she holds her tongue.

"How about you, Prince Zev?" Rivelis asks the werewolf with a small smile, while Zev looks a bit shocked that he's being addressed directly. "Wouldn't you like the slaughtering to end?"

"More than anything, Your Highness."

"Then let me mull our options while you all rest.

Rune, show our guests to the western madrone lofts. The Celebration of the Sun begins tomorrow, and you'll have an excellent view of the festivities."

"We'll have clothes brought to the rooms," Scocha says with a smile. I goddamn love this fae family.

Rune gives a quick bow, then turns to us and gestures toward the door. The large group of guards that walked us in here no longer has the job of escorting us around, and the sneer on Eliar's face shows that he doesn't love it.

I, on the other hand, am thrilled to feel like an honored guest and not a prisoner. I might get some rest and enjoy myself for a day. Except that my baby's off in the woods somewhere, hiding out. And my lover is still at the very beginning of his three-day torture sentence. Perhaps my mind isn't going to let me just enjoy these comforts.

On the way out, Rune stops in front of his cousin and holds out his hand expectantly. A moment later, and with a look of pure resentment, Eliar hands my wand to the fae prince, who in turn passes it to me. I give Eliar the absolute sassiest smile on my way out.

Rune leads us down a couple of tree flights after we leave the royal chamber, then we start across a long bridge made of ivy vines that runs between tree-tops. We're high enough up that I can see a lake in the distance, and a nearby hilltop that's covered in grapevines and fruit trees. I can't turn my head without being charmed to death by Aevelairith.

We finally reach our rooms, which are quaint little yurts at the end of individual walkways atop a massive madrone. I'm reminded of the fancy tropical resorts, where you have your own room at the end of a dock over the water. Instead of being over the water, these rooms stand over an entire forest.

We each have our own space, and in mine I find a plush four poster bed draped with colorful silks, a sitting area with a loveseat and two chairs made of wood so supple and carved so beautifully that when I sit on one I don't even miss the cushions. There's an armoire with a decorative depiction of a large tree with roots that run down to the floor, a bathroom complete with a tub, a fancy looking toilet and a shiny mirror to show just how shitty I looked when I met the king and queen of the fae. Throughout the space are open windows, letting in the fresh evening air carrying a hint of lavender. Hanging in my wardrobe is a beautiful yellow and green gown in just my size. I'm not all that big on dresses, but this one just falls over my body in the most comfortable way.

"Eff me, this thing fits like a dream!"

AJ's voice is a little piercing, but I appreciate that

she's having the same dress-wearing experience as I am.

There's a knock at my door and I turn to see Zev and Rune waiting at the entrance. They are both dressed in the simple yet elegant style of the fae, with fitted vests edged with gold and silver leaves. Zev comes to me first, taking me in his arms and admiring my new threads. After a tender kiss, I pull from my mate's arms and walk over to hug Rune.

"Of all the magic I've seen, this place might be the most magical," I say. "And your parents are, like, parents."

Rune smiles, then looks to Zev. "The werewolves have seen a different side of them from time to time, but our familial connection is strong."

He pauses, throwing a quick glance at the door before looking into my eyes. "I felt compelled to lie about Rain because I don't trust everyone's intentions just yet. My cousin is a fine example of the more hostile members of our kingdom, who perhaps aren't ready for this war to end, and certainly aren't ready to believe the prophecy has a different interpretation."

I nod and hug him again, showing my understanding and siphoning off his calming energy. I'm glad he lied about my baby's whereabouts and I'm feeling more confident now that she's safe with Erzsébet. Food, shelter and warmth won't be an issue as long as she's with Granny Witch.

I look out the window, taking in the alluring view and breathing in the sweet, clean air.

"What's the Celebration of the Sun?" I ask.

Rune moves over to my side, equally enamored by the sight of his homeland. "It's a month-long celebration at the end of our Spring. The days grow longer until we reach a day without darkness. Starting tomorrow, the royal family hosts a feast each day as the fae bring the Spring bounty to share with one another. During these years fraught with battle, this month has been a lone bright spot in Aevelairith."

Zev joins us at the window and puts his arm around Rune's shoulder instead of mine. It's a bit of a surprise, but my heart flutters at the show of affection between the two.

"I fear the wolves may have ruined a celebration or two, my friend."

Rune responds to the touch by leaning his head down, resting it sweetly against Zev's. "And we did the same or worse to you."

It's all I can do not to turn into a blubbering baby. I imagine if a civil war had broken out in Mass and somehow AJ and I ended up on opposite sides. It seems like an impossibility that we'd turn against each other, but I'm not so naive to assume everything would be peachy.

"Did you guys try to stay friends when it all started?" This level of intimacy between the two has me feeling bolder than normal about diving into these old wounds. They turn to face me, keeping their arms around each other's shoulders.

"For years," Zev answers. "At the beginning, we considered the four of us the great hope for a united future."

"Cara's death broke our connection with Darius," Rune says. "After that, we didn't see or speak with him until arriving at your bar. Zev and I lost touch a few years later."

I'm about to ask more, yearning to learn every detail about these men I love, but Rune's eyes shoot up to the entryway and his mood changes. I spin to follow his gaze and find his sister standing in the doorway.

She walks in, eyes darting between each of us, and closes the door behind her.

"I didn't get a chance to say hello, Revia," Zev says with a slight smirk. I'm sure these two have some sort of history, and the princess's response makes me think it's not all great.

"I don't fold as easily as my father," she snaps, then brushes past Zev to face her brother.

"You've brought a wolf into our most sacred rooms, and the Last Witch is here in Aevelairith." She punctuates this statement with a look at me, and it's clear that I had some sort of tell when Rune told his little fib in the royal chamber.

"I know you've told lies, and I need to know how many," she goes on, her gaze back on Rune. "Give me the truth, or I'll have all of your friends killed."

CHAPTER ELEVEN

Rune and Revia are locked in a tense staredown, while Zev and I stay watchful, showing no reaction to the threat against our lives. That doesn't mean inside I'm not bristling like an angry porcupine. Our peaceful stay in the fae realm has taken a quick and unexpected turn.

"I'm a little surprised by your hostility, Revia," Rune says.

"You shouldn't be. Perhaps your time off in another world, forming bonds with sworn enemies has made you forget the needs of our people and the crimes of others." She doesn't need to look at Zev on that last line for us to know who she's talking about.

"Lest we forget our own crimes," Rune says. "And

perhaps you're right, time away has changed my mind on some things, but only because I had a chance to realize our reading of an ancient prophecy is flawed at best."

"On what grounds? Everything else has come true, Rune. The three kingdoms are locked in eternal war. We are losing the strength of our magic. Our numbers have dwindled as our mothers cannot bear children. You've fallen in love with a witch and suddenly decided the prophecy has no merit. Tell me I'm wrong."

Rune hesitates and looks at me. I know that I love him, but something about his sister accusing him of *falling* in love with me puts a whole new spin on our relationship.

"Yet everything you mention stems from the death of the witches. As their power has been extinguished, so has our own. The prophecy felt valid because we made it so. And might I ask, what magic do you think will be unlocked by killing an innocent child?" Rune now has a little more edge on his voice than before. "What other fae rituals fall in line with killing an infant? How far outside your moral code are you willing to step for a contested interpretation?"

Revia again turns to me, but the anger in her eyes

has turned to concern. I don't think she likes the idea of taking an innocent life. Rune's framing might have her rethinking things.

She takes a moment and then changes the topic when she speaks. "Where is the child? I know she's alive and I don't believe she's on Earth."

I can tell Rune's thinking of how best to play this. Sell the lie or see if the truth will set us free? I'm not surprised when he opts for the latter.

"Yes, she is here. She's with the queen witch, hidden somewhere on the edges of the valley. You won't find her unless Bernadette wants her to be found, however."

Revia considers this thoughtfully. She came in with a full head of steam, but the sincerity of her brother seems to have her on a different track.

"It was wise to keep that from our parents, I think. Knowing the Last Witch was within the realm might cloud their vision."

"It seemed like the safest version of our story," Rune says.

The siblings share a pensive moment, and I see the similarities in them. Rune might be on the calmer side, but I think that comes with being the younger child without the same pressure of leading.

"I'm sorry for the threat," Revia says. "These have

been difficult times, and battles haven't stopped while you were away. Until today, I was expecting the vampires would stage an attack during Celebration, as they often do." She raises an eyebrow and looks to Zev. "Now I only have to worry about the wolves it would seem."

"If they come, I'll fight by your side, princess," my wolf says in response. Revia smiles, then heads for the door.

"Such strange times. It's nice to see you, brother. And welcome to Aevelairith, Bernadette."

She takes the tension in the room with her when she leaves, and I sink onto the bed, exhausted by... everything.

I miss my daughter, but I know she's safer wherever she is.

I worry about Darius, and I have to constantly shift my thoughts away from imagining what unthinkable loneliness and despair he's enduring.

The guys are standing side by side, staring out the window as the sun sets completely and the moon rises full in the sky, letting in moonbeams that cast shimmering rays of silver light across my room.

"I feel the pull of the full moon," Zev says, speaking gruffly. "I must shift."

Rune frowns. "There will be patrols everywhere. You won't be safe in wolf form."

Zev looks meaningfully at the fae. "I will be safe. I know how to evade your kind, brother. And being back in my homeworld on a full moon, I have no choice."

Rune nods and Zev comes over to me and pulls me from the bed into his arms. His kiss is bruising and passionate and I can feel his wolf at the surface, ready to come out and play. How I wish I could go running through the woods with him. I feel the call of it in my blood as his mate, but have no outlet for that impulse.

When he pulls away, his nails already growing and his body shifting, I feel the absence, and I watch in awe as his fancy fae clothes are shredded in his shift from man to wolf.

I'll be keeping an eye on you. We can't trust everyone here. Call if you need me.

His parting words give me a small comfort, knowing he'll be out there if anything happens.

I'm just hoping nothing happens. One night of no one trying to kill me would be super fab.

Zev leaps through an open window in a fluid motion born of instinct and disappears into the woods. I still feel our connection, our mate bond singing through my blood, which eases my anxiety.

I turn to Rune, whose eyes are trained on the horizon beyond our rooms, when AJ bursts in. "Yo. Did Zev just wolf out in the middle of enemy territory?"

"He's fine," I say with more conviction than I feel.

Oh come now, love. Have more faith in me than that.

I cringe that Zev felt my uncertainty.

It's not you I doubt.

AJ yawns and glances down at her pendant. Her lips purse like she's about to say something about it until she notices me watching.

She yawns again, this time with way more exaggeration. "I'm wiped. Heading to bed." She grins at Rune and me. "Don't do anything I wouldn't do."

I snort. "That leaves a lot on the table."

"Exactly. Have fun," she says in a sing-songy voice as she leaves, closing the door behind her.

I glance at Rune, who is now watching me with such intensity I blush. Then I feel stupid for blushing, given this guy helped me birth my child and has already seen me at my most vulnerable.

"You must be tired," Rune says, though he makes no move to leave.

"Not as much as I thought," I say as my heartbeat escalates until I can hear the whoosh of my own blood.

Rune steps closer to me and takes my hand in his. "I apologize for how my cousin treated you. I should have done more."

He glances away, the mood that was building between us fizzling like dying soap bubbles. "It wasn't your fault," I say. "And your parents laid into him publicly. Almost made it all worth it."

"I'm relieved they were welcoming. I was worried," he says.

"I know. But it must be nice to be home?" My voice lands on a hopeful note and he smiles and brushes a stray hair from my face with his free hand.

"It is. But as I'm sure you know, homecoming is always a mixed bag."

"I feel that," I say. "I'm surprised your parents weren't more committed to killing my baby," I say, then flinch at how badly those words came out of my mouth. But Rune doesn't seem bothered.

"In truth, I am as well. Something must have happened while I was gone to soften their stance on this, but I can't imagine what. We still don't have a final answer, so we'll have to see how this ends. They will speak with other fae leaders, including my sister, who may not be in favor of allying with enemies who killed so many of our brothers and sisters."

We both walk out onto the balcony and sit on the bench facing the vista. A sky full of stars set like diamonds against velvet, the moon hanging heavy overhead, casting the world around us in an ethereal glow. Rune slips an arm over my shoulder and I lean into him as we continue our conversation.

"It feels like the fae will make or break this alliance," I say, speaking the truth we both know all too well. It would be hard for the wolves to say no when both the vampires and fae were in agreement against all odds. Without the fae, the wolves have much less reason to trust the vampires alone.

"Zev will secure the wolves," Rune says, and I hear the message he's not saying out loud. There is a way Zev can secure allyship with his kingdom... if he's king.

I lean forward and rub my temples, as the beginning of a headache sneaks up on me. "What exactly is happening in this world that you each thought the prophecy and my baby could fix?" I ask as Rune rubs my sore back with his strong, skilled hands.

"The magic is fading. Procreation has all but

stopped. Vampires can no longer turn others except the king himself. Our races will die out if we do not reverse it."

"Right, you mentioned that. But what does that look like specifically? How do you know it's because magic is dying and not because, I don't know, people are taking the wrong meds?"

He pauses his ministrations on my back as he thinks. I would have asked a less riveting question if I knew it meant he'd stop massaging me with those exquisite hands.

I twist to face him and he takes both my hands in his. "I want to show you something, if you don't mind?"

I nod, expecting us to slip into his memories like before. But instead, he stands, pulling me up with him. Rather than jump out the window like Zev, we leave via the door and down through winding trails and thick trees that glow a luminescent green in the night.

In fact, between the full moon and how much of the foliage around us has that graceful glow, I don't need a light to see just fine.

We hike together in companionable silence, holding hands, and I take in as much of the intoxicating fae evening as I can. The air is thick with the scent of lavender and something else… something sweet. It's a balmy evening, and part of me thinks the weather here is always some version of perfect. I can feel the bite of chill in the air that still speaks of warmer days to come.

"It's incredible to me, how all the plant life glows," I say, and he pauses to turn to me with an intrigued look.

"You can see it?"

"Uh, yeah. It's hard to miss. How do you think I'm able to see in the dark?" I ask.

He looks past me, lost in thought for a moment. "What you're seeing is the life flow of the plant kingdom. Their spirits. All my life, I've only known fae to see their true nature." He shrugs, his expression still a bit vacant and turns to continue walking.

I don't know what to make of his words. "Maybe when the queen of trees stabbed me, I got some kind of new plant super power?" I ask.

He tilts his head, pondering it. "Perhaps."

He doesn't sound convinced, but whatever it is, I enjoy the walk through what feels like pure magic.

It seems very sudden when we stop at an impossibly tall gate to a massive garden. Towering stone walls stand before us covered in vines dotted with glowing silver orbs.

"How did I not see this until now?" I ask, looking behind me. I should have been able to see it for the last ten minutes of our walk.

"It is part of the magic of this place. You'll understand in a moment."

He places his palm into a hand shaped mold on the door. Something clicks and Rune pulls his hand back, wiping blood off his palm as he does.

Slowly the door grunts and grinds open, sounding as if it hasn't budged in eons.

When we step into the garden, I become more convinced no one has been here in a super long time.

It's an incredible and wildly overgrown paradise of lush trees, crystal growths glimmering iridescent, blue, red, wild flowers letting off the fragrant scent I could smell even back in my room. In the center of it all, a massive tree that towers over the rest, branches spread thick and long, roots clearly going deep and wide through the earth.

Everything in the garden is alive and glows with that magic I shouldn't be able to see... everything except the mighty tree.

I suck in my breath and step forward, holding my

hand out. I place my palm on the tree and squeeze back tears at the emptiness I feel from it. "What happened to her?" I ask, feeling very strongly this was not just an ordinary tree. Though it is nearly fossilized, I can still sense what once was within.

"She is the Tree of Life. The epicenter of magical harmony in our world. As you can see, she is dying. Perhaps she is already dead and the magic she left behind just takes longer to disappear entirely. Either way, without her, all of this world will slowly perish."

"And everyone thought sacrificing Rain would wake her back up?"

Rune doesn't glance away from my harsh tone, instead he holds my gaze and nods.

"She doesn't want blood," I say, feeling into something I don't quite understand. "Not the way you think."

This gets the fae's attention, and he is immediately by my side, almost as fast as Darius. "Can you hear her? My grandmother said the tree spoke to the royals, once upon a time. Do you know how to bring her to life?"

There's so much hope in his voice, I feel I'll crush him when I tell him the truth. "I don't. All I know is she doesn't want what you think she wants."

I let my hands fall away, knowing I'll get nothing more from her and it will just be frustrating to try.

Whatever part of my power is letting me see plant souls and talk to trees is still very much a training wheel gift. I don't really know what the hell I'm doing.

Rune cups my face in his hand and I glance up at him. "Do not feel bad for not having answers to questions that three long-lived races have been asking for centuries."

"Well, when you put it like that..." It doesn't mean I'm not going to feel bad that I can't do more. That I've inadvertently brought so much chaos and death to this world, a world I didn't even know about two months ago. That said, I'll shed any sense of guilt for a moment and just enjoy being in this magic garden with this magic man.

The wind ripples around us, caressing our skin and Rune's silver eyes become pools I get lost in as he gazes so lovingly at me. "Oh Bernie..."

I lose my patience and grab the back of his head, pulling his lips to mine as I stand on the balls of my feet to reach his mouth.

The passion that infects us with this kiss is nothing like we have experienced before with each other.

It can't be compared to anything I've experienced ever. It's like lightning striking my soul, cracking me open and filling me with the most extraordinary burst of energy. I'm blinded by the light that burns through us as our bodies press together, and the world around us disappears.

An urgency grips us and we run our hands over each other as if we might never feel the touch of a lover again.

The moonlight guides us, and Rune's skin glows just like the plants and flowers. His eyes alight with silver, his skin dusted with diamonds.

We undress each other slowly, forestalling our own desperate need to touch, to bind our bodies to each other. When we both stand naked under the moon, the plants and flowers around us seem to light up even brighter, casting a glow over our bare flesh and somehow amplifying our desire.

Rune lays me on the lush carpet-like expanse of grass under the Tree of Life and holds himself up over me as his lips and hands continue to explore my body, memorizing the taste and feel of my skin. His long hair tickles at my breasts as he moves down... down... down...

And I lose myself in his touch. In the feel of him. In the ecstasy of emotion that overtakes me at his closeness, his energy that merges and blends with mine as our bodies come together.

When he enters me, my magic curls around him like he's part of me, and we are held together by the tethers of my power as we move as one.

When we reach the edge of our pleasure, we topple over together and into delirious flight. I have one hand around him, fingernails digging into his muscular back, and one hand clutching the earth, my magic shooting out of me as the waves of climax continue to rock me.

Rune collapses next to me, keeping us close as we both catch our breath, and I spare a glance for the tree, hoping my surge of power didn't kill anything in the garden. Instead, it looks as though it did the exact opposite. For a fleeting second, the Tree of Life has a subtle, almost imperceptible glow.

As the light from my magic quickly fades from the grass, I'm startled by the sound of a deep sigh.

I turn to Rune, eyes wide. "Did you hear that?"

He blinks at me, clearly still lost in the pleasure of our coupling. "Hear what?"

I shrug and tuck myself into his arms, laying my head on his chest. "Nothing. I must have imagined it."

We don't intend to fall asleep under the tree and stay there all night, but that's exactly what we do.

And in the morning, as the sun rises, casting the garden in a golden light, I awake to the sound of a wolf's howl.

CHAPTER TWELVE

Love, hurry back to the rooms. The king and queen have requested counsel.

I communicate to Rune what Zev said, and we both dress quickly and stand to leave. Before we get to the gate, I turn back to look at the Tree of Life one last time, as if she called my name. There's the hint of a whisper on the wind, but then it's gone and I'm not sure if I really heard it to begin with.

I turn away from the magical garden and head to our rooms with Rune. Zev is there waiting for us, shifted back to human form but apparently he hasn't bothered to find clothes.

"You know, given how often one of us appears buck naked in front of Rune's parents, they're going to think we're running some kind of nudist colony," I say, before mentally adding, *though I certainly am not complaining about the view.*

He gives me a little growl, then draws in a long breath through his nose. I know what he's smelling, and it's made even clearer as he looks between me and Rune. My emotions creep toward nervousness but then dance back. I don't know if I'll ever be able to explain the understanding that exists between my trio of lovers, and how I can continue to love each of them more without loving any of them less. I'm half-convinced I've got a bunch of separate hearts in my chest, each devoted to another person. And then a final, bigger heart for my baby, who's hopefully off having a magical time in a cave or something.

AJ joins us, looking exquisite in a flowery skirt-- literally made of flowers--and a fluffy sweater. Whoever runs the fae fashion department is nailing it and deserves a raise.

"We going to see the king and queen? And then maybe somewhere for lunch?"

Rune smiles, enjoying the strange bit of our world AJ is bringing to his. "To the royal chamber, yes. Then we'll eat, either to celebrate good news or decide what to do next."

Zev finally succumbs to the social pressure of wearing clothing, and the four of us head off, the rope bridges and branch walkways as charming this morning as they were last night. For this walk, however, my tiredness is replaced with anxiety. Last night felt hopeful, but things can change. Minds can change. They almost always do. And it certainly can't be an easy decision to align with enemies who have been killing your people for so long.

When we walk into the sprawling, wooden hall, Rivelis and Scocha immediately stand from their thrones. Revia stays seated, which seems as good an indicator as any of what's to come.

"How was your sleep?" the queen asks, looking mostly at me but I assume addressing the group.

"Freaking bliss," AJ answers first.

"Yeah, it was wonderful," I say. "Your kingdom is just... indescribable."

"Thank you," Rivelis says. "We agree, and we have battled with all our might to protect our home. Which is why..."

This guy gets straight to the point, which is very refreshing after meeting so many powerful people who like to speak in riddles.

"The timing seems right for a change in

approach," the king continues. "I have every appre-hension about an alliance, and I know very little about this new enemy. But I trust my son. And I believe in a new interpretation of the prophecy, since every past step has only pushed us closer to the brink. We've been caught in a self-defeating cycle and I'm ready to break free. Rune, Bernadette--you have the commitment of the fae."

AJ hoots, fist in the air and everything.

I suppress a smile as relief washes over me. Though it felt like a win last night, nothing is ever guaranteed.

Revia finally stands and comes forward with a forced smile. "I trust, brother, that you'll have treaties ready for ratification in the coming days. Abnormal as this situation may be, there must be some normalcy of process."

Rune nods, but his words belie his body language. "There's no time for a political approach, Revia. Timót's army did to the vampires in a matter of minutes what our kind could not do in centuries of war. We either go on the offensive immediately or die waiting."

"Buzzkill," AJ mutters under her breath. The tone has taken a considerably negative turn.

The king looks upward, twirling his fingers in his long beard. "What, then, is the first step? I'll agree to an alliance, but I won't welcome the other races into our kingdom first."

"That's fair and wise," Rune says. "I trust the commitment of the vampires, and of our brother in pledge, Darius. We'll return by portal to Vaemor as soon as we've gathered our things."

The king and queen's faces drop a little. So does AJ's, as she was dead set on eating some delicious fae food and probably has a little PTSD from her waterless experience in the vampire realm.

"Will you not stay for the first night of the festival?" Queen Scocha asks. "I think it will be important to have the entire family present for the opening feast. A show of solidarity before we announce such a striking change of course."

"If I may," Revia cuts in, "I think they should move on as quickly as possible, if what Rune says is true about this stranger and his army of dragons."

"Revia's right," Rune says, but I butt into the conversation with a point he may have forgotten.

"Actually, there's one reason we might want to stay. Aside from another night in a bed and a delicious meal, we still have to wait on Darius. He's got at least another night in the Tomb and the vampires won't move while he's still serving."

All the royals look at me, unaware of this news.

"They've put your friend in the Tomb of Time?" the king asks.

"As punishment for betraying the vampire cause," Zev offers, speaking for the first time and causing a lot of heads to whip his way in surprise. I can sense he's being tactical--using his position as an outsider to speak about another non-fae--and trying to show the unity of the three princes. "He went willingly."

There's a moment of silence, this news seeming to weigh heavily on the king and queen. I kinda wish Rune had offered it up last night, might have saved us all the hours of waiting.

"Well," Rivelis says at last, "then it is settled. You will stay and enjoy the first night of celebration before returning to Vaemor in the morning."

Rune smiles in agreement as Queen Scocha tries to hide her excitement. I'm just as happy; even though we have dragons to kill and werewolves to win over, I'll let all of that wait one more night. I need more time with Rune in his kingdom, seeing his true self surrounded by impeccable beauty.

The king looks like he's about to say something

else when Revia quickly bows and exits through a doorway in the back of the chamber. It seems a little abrupt, but I don't know anything about how anything works in this royal family--or any royal family for that matter, though I have read an impressive number of articles about the British royal family and the Queen. Still, I doubt this family has rules about which shoes the women in the family must wear.

"I'm sure she's off to oversee preparations," Scocha says, then looks at me. "The first night of the Celebration spares no expense."

The king and queen bow to us and we do the same in return--even Zev, after refusing to lower his head an inch in the vampire kingdom. Either he's got a better relationship with the fae or he's softening to this whole alliance thing.

As we leave, I sneak a quick, hushed conversation with Rune. "Is it safe to try and find Rain?" I assume it is, but I'd rather not bring up Rune's lie in front of anyone else.

He thinks for a moment, then takes my hand as he shakes his head. The mixture of his calming energy and my sadness leaves me feeling pretty neutral.

"The situation is volatile enough without exploring my dishonesty. We'll find them on the way to the portal tomorrow."

And I'll track the witch queen and check in with them tonight, Zev says in my mind, offering a true bit of comfort. If I can get word that they're safe, I'll rest much easier.

Before going back to our rooms, Rune takes us down to a river outside the main gate. It looks like it's full of beaver dams, but a closer look shows each little mound of sticks is actually a different food vendor. It's like taco trucks, but waterside huts that actually float along the water. Rune plays the royalty card and we get samples of everything, from fresh fish to fruit to baked goods. Most of the food I've never seen before but would happily eat until I die. It's the best lunch I've had in ages, if not ever. The only problem is listening to AJ yell "MMMMMMM" after every single bite.

At one point she asks if eating a fish taco is considered cannibalism now that she has fins. No one validates the question with a response, and she has no problem shrugging off the moral conundrum as she decimates the fish, inhaling it like a starving person.

Once our tummies are full, we walk along the river until we reach a small cave that a section of the river channels into. Rune steps into the water then ducks into the entrance. We all follow, our hands reaching out to keep us steady as light gives way to darkness. A few steps into the cave, a sparkling blue light illuminates every wall, turning it into a magical, glowing cavern. The river widens into a swimming hole with narrow rock platforms along the edge of the water for people to stand or sit.

AJ is immediately out of her clothes and swimming, this time keeping a bra on but losing the pants so her fins can wiggle free.

"There are caves like this all along the river," Rune says as he strips down. "Enough that you can almost always find one with privacy."

He dives in, swimming deep into the water below. Zev comes over and puts his arm around me, whispering into my ear and making my skin turn into a field of goosebumps.

"Some real privacy would be nice," he says. "A night away from you makes me need you so much more."

I turn toward him and capture his lips with mine, also taking the opportunity to reach down and give a quick tease with my hand. "I've been needing you, too. Will you have to shift again tonight?"

He moans at my touch and growls at his reality, making it clear he'll be off in wolf form after the banquet instead of wrapped in my arms.

"Another night, then," he says. "When we get to my kingdom, expect to be properly ravaged."

I feel his rigid member for a moment longer, until we both might cave, then dive into the water. Seconds later I hear him splash in after me.

As I swim away, I feel another set of hands trace along the sides of my ribcage, and the pleasing touch makes clear it's Rune. I spin toward him, smiling underwater at his beautiful face, warmed by the smile he gives me in return. I'll miss Zev tonight, but I'm already stirring with the anticipation of another night with my fae prince.

I give Rune a kiss and then head for the surface to catch my breath. When I break through the water, I see AJ sitting on one of the rock ledges, her tail dangling into the river below. She's got a sweet but almost melancholic look on her face and I see that she's staring at her little pendant again. I throw a glance back at the Sexies swimming behind me, and they take the hint that I'm heading off for some girl time.

I swim over and climb out to sit by her side. She tries to tuck the pendant away, but she's too much of a fish and doesn't have pockets.

"No more sneakiness, A. Where did you get that and why are you obsessing over it like Gollum?"

"You know how I feel about Gollum, B," AJ says with sincere admonishment. Always the contrarian, AJ decided when we were younger that Gollum was the true hero of The Lord of the Rings since he never let the ring fall into the wrong hands. It's complicated, but she's got a whole theory and I guarantee she was talking about it most nights while running Morgan's.

"Right, sorry. Also, don't change the subject."

"You're going to make fun of me," AJ says, staring at the pendant with a blush in her cheeks.

"When have I ever made fun of you?" I say back.

She thinks for a second, then laughs. "Fair point. I guess, if I were you I'd make fun of me." She takes a deep breath, sucking in some vulnerability, then proceeds. "It's, um, from the ghost. In the bar, the one you summoned or whatever. He didn't give it to me because he's a freaking invisible ghost, but he told me where to find it, down in your cellar."

"So... it's Tilly's? Or Ed's?" It's okay if AJ keeps something that belonged to my grandparents, but I want to know if this ghost is giving away stuff that isn't his to give.

"No, no, the ghost--his name is Leo, by the way, so hot--he brought it through from his... from the other side. He can touch and carry things there, but it's a lot harder in the living world. He's explained it all but it's pretty complicated."

"I bet. So what's the deal?"

AJ looks longingly at the pendant. "He says he can live inside here so... Jesus, it sounds cheesy AF when I say it out loud--so we can always be together."

It would sound cheesy, but I know it means something to AJ and there's nothing sappy about it. A couple weeks with this invisible dead man in my bar has really changed something in her.

"Hell, AJ, you finally find a guy who isn't trash and he's already dead."

"I know, right?" The tragedy of the situation isn't lost on her. "Still, I can hear him through this, and he can hear me." AJ stops, emotions catching in her throat and forcing a pause before she can continue. "He whispered to me the whole time you were gone, when I was paralyzed in the vampire place. I swear to God, B, I'd have died from insanity if he wasn't there."

Her story rips me apart and I bring her in for a hug so we can both do a little crying. I can't wait to get back to the bar and try to figure out a way to bring this Leo guy back from the dead. If it means giving AJ the man she deserves, I'll break into some dark magic.

After a moment of reflection, we're both ready to dive back into the sparkling water. The four of us swim around, enjoying a type of calm we haven't had in so long. I can't give into it fully, though. Whenever I get close I think first of Rain, then of Darius. There's no way to be completely happy without them near me.

The swimming eventually winds down, and only AJ is left splashing and frolicking with her impressive tail. We all get out, dry off, dress and head back into the kingdom. Rune says the festival starts in the late afternoon and carries on through the evening, so everyone has time to rest up before a night of revelry.

I'm balancing my sadness at missing Rain and worrying about Darius with my excitement at having a night of fun and celebration.

Even after a good night's sleep, I still hit the mattress like a sack of potatoes and power nap as soon as we get back. My dreams are practically the same as the reality I'm living, only with my baby by my side. I splash with her in the water and lay her down on a blanket in the middle of a grassy field. She's absolutely coming to Aevelairith for the Celebration of the Sun each year.

I'm left feeling a bit empty when I wake up, having such vivid dreams of my child and then finding her gone again. I remind myself that it's okay, she's with the most powerful woman in the universe, and it's nice to have a few nights off. Rain's probably happy to be away from me for a little while, since all I do is traipse her from one dangerous place to the next.

More clothes have been delivered when I wake up. The same must be true for AJ, because her yelling "DAMN!" is actually what wakes me up. I've got a short dress with a swirling pattern of purple and green, a scoop neck and three quarter length sleeves with a tasteful frill around the edges.

AJ bursts in and we both squeal with delight to see our dresses are matching, with hers in pink and blue. Zev and Rune come in to see what the fuss is about, and they both look dashing in similar worn leather pants and silk shirts. If they were going to a cocktail party on Earth it might be too much; for the Celebration of the Sun in the fae world, it's just right.

A selfish part of me longs for Darius to be in our company, but I know tensions would shoot through the roof if there was a vampire in the land. There's a lot of animosity the fae will have to overcome for the races to join forces, so it's best to take these changes in small doses.

Darius is no small dose.

Rune leads us from our rooms to a stone walkway on the ground floor, heading toward a part of the kingdom we haven't seen yet. The path is lined with tall flowers that sway in a non-existent wind, moving on their own to absorb the final rays of dusk's sunlight.

I notice other fae walking along parallel paths, heading toward the same open meadow. When we reach the gathering, it's like a classy carnival. There are food carts and games and musicians and jugglers; a man rides by on what looks like a short giraffe; colorful birds flutter around us, ready to pick the ground clean of food.

It's a fun, casual version of magic and I love it.

As we move through the crowd, we see a long, ovular table, with the king, queen and princess sitting behind it. Other people sit around the table eating as well, and it seems like the purpose is to mingle the royal family with the rest of their people. Rivelis and Scocha smile and chat with anyone who comes near, while Revia has her usual, distant look.

"Let me speak with the king and queen, then we'll walk the grounds more," Rune says, giving my arm a gentle touch before heading off.

"Let's go eat everything," AJ says. She's always had an appetite, but I think maybe this new mermaid thing has her burning calories faster. She ate like a linebacker at lunch and now she's ready for more.

"Yes, please," Zev says, looking extra hungry with a night of wolf-prowling on his mind.

"You two go ahead, I'll wait for Rune and then catch up."

I get a kiss from my mate and a wink from AJ and then they're off, leaving me to take in the scene. I'm enamored with all of it--the way the fae look and conduct themselves, the world they live in, the food they eat, the plants they grow. I would do a lot to save this kingdom, these people. Rune's family. Almost anything. Anything except sacrificing my child. That's a few steps too far. In the thought exercise where your child gets stuck in the gears needed to lift a bridge and if you don't lift it, a boat full of people will die, what do you do? Save your child and sacrifice the boat full of people? Or kill your child to save them? I'll always pick my kid. Star Trek's original Spock might have judged me for that choice. But end-of-life Spock would have understood. The needs of the many do not always outweigh the needs of the one or the few.

"Lost your clan?"

It's not exactly the voice I wanted to hear, and I turn to see Eliar standing behind me.

"I'm fine, thank you."

"Forgive me if we got off on the wrong foot," he says, extending his hand. "You can appreciate that unwelcome visitors have long been a source of anguish, and, well…"

He leaves it at that, not needing to say more. I put my hand in his and allow him to give a courteous peck just above the knuckles. It seems harmless enough, but then he pulls me into him and presses against me. There are people all around, but he sways like we're dancing and doesn't cause enough of a scene to catch anyone's eye.

"You need to let go of me," I say through gritted teeth, offering the only warning he's going to get.

"I've heard you humans love fae," Eliar says with a lecherous smile. "I happen to love foreign women, so this should work out fine."

I've got my wand strapped to my thigh so it's hidden under my dress, and I'm trying to think of a way to discreetly grab it and turn this piece of shit into a beetle. But before I can make a move, Rune sticks a hand between us, grabs Eliar by the chest, lifts him off his feet and slams him onto his back. While the unwanted advance didn't get anyone's attention, this encounter surely does.

"You're not worthy of the air she breathes, much

less the touch of her body," Rune says, a fire in his eyes like I've never seen before.

Eliar's eyes are still wide and he returns the fiery stare. "Careful, Rune. There's still a lot of doubt as to which side you're on."

More fae have stopped to watch the scuffle. I think Rune senses that as he hoists Eliar back to his feet and gives him a firm, faux-friendly pat on the shoulder.

"The same could probably be said about you, cousin. Go enjoy the festival, and perhaps go light on the drink."

Eliar gives me one last look before briskly walking off. Rune watches him go, then turns to me.

"Are you alright?" he asks, the fire in his gaze turned to love and concern.

"Yeah, nothing happened. He's just an idiot."

Rune nods, looking me over as though there might be an emotional injury I missed.

"War brings out the worst in us. I'm glad we may have a chance to end it."

He takes my hand and leads me off to see more wonders of the festival. We find AJ and Zev a few minutes later, both greedily eating some kind of kabob. I sample half a dozen fruit wines, we play a strange game where you throw beans into a Venus flytrap, and AJ and Zev split another sandwich.

As the moon grows brighter, Zev bids us all adieu, sneaking off to become a wolf before the need becomes too great. We share a long kiss behind a food stand, each getting a little handsier than is suitable for public, and then he sprints into the darkness, beginning his shift just before he's out of sight.

I walk back to AJ and Rune, and I'm almost lost in the joy of the moment. I feel like everyone is, even just for this brief flash of time, safe. There's nothing else I ought to be doing. It's okay that I'm here and I'm allowed to enjoy myself. It's a very relieving feeling.

And then there's a scream.

Bloodcurdling, coming from the direction of the main table.

Rune sprints toward the sound without hesitation, and AJ and I are a step or two behind.

All of the guests have frozen, looking toward the same spot, and I'm terrified and confused by the sight when it finally comes into view.

The king and queen still sit at their table, but their heads have dropped to their plates. Scocha's wine glass has toppled over, and the contents mix with the red blood trickling from her nose. Rivelis is in the same position, blood pooling below his ear.

Revia stands over them, staring back at us.

Just as I start to wonder what happened, what she's done, she raises her finger and points at Rune.

"Traitor!"

CHAPTER THIRTEEN

There's silence throughout the kingdom.

All eyes are on Rune, waiting for him to speak. He looks between his lifeless parents and his sister, his hands balled into fists. He's trying to maintain some calm, but I can see he's starting to tremble.

"Revia…"

"Don't deny what you have done!" the princess screams. "You chose a witch over the fae. You side with the vampires now. Tell everyone, Rune. Tell them of your choices."

Guards have started to form a circle around us. I hear footsteps a few feet behind me and there's not a doubt in my mind it's Eliar.

This is all very coordinated. Rune's done nothing

wrong and had the blessing of the king and queen, but they're not alive to say so.

Revia killed her own parents to foil our plans.

What's she willing to do to her brother?

I'm not about to find out, and I can only hope Rune's on the same page. I spin around, grabbing my wand from my Tomb Raider-style thigh holster and blasting Eliar in the chest all in one fluid motion. The moment the light leaves my wand, Rune puts up an illusion that covers everything and everyone in thick white mist.

I instantly feel like it's harder to breathe, even though it's not real and can't possibly be impeding my airways. The mind is a crazy powerful thing, but it's also easily fooled it would seem.

AJ grabs my right arm, leaving my hand free to keep my wand at the ready, and Rune reaches for my left hand, guiding us out of his illusion as I hear guards scramble to find us.

I have no idea where we're going and can't see a damn thing, but that should mean they can't see us either. Unless playing this game with fae is like a child thinking that closing their own eyes will render them invisible to others.

I trust Rune knows what he's doing. He wouldn't create an illusion that didn't work.

Nevertheless, I've got fire spells on the tip of my tongue.

There's commotion everywhere, and I feel bodies brushing by us while I continue to follow Rune's lead. I have to assume none of the people I bump into are guards, because I really don't want to hurt an innocent fae. While I can't see, it seems like we're moving against the flow of traffic. Hopefully that means anyone looking for us is going in the opposite direction as well.

Rune winds us through the mist until we reach a solid stone wall. I only know because I walk right into it before Rune can stop me.

He pulls on something--I can't see what--and a secret passage opens. The three of us slip into a dark opening, the door closes on us and the mist disappears.

In the silence, with only the tip of my wand giving us light, I throw myself into Rune's arms, tears I've been holding back leaking down my cheeks. The sadness hits me like a tidal wave, and I think I'm channeling Rune's feelings as well as my own, though he's remaining much more stoic than me.

He squeezes me tightly, nods brusquely and then pulls away. Through his touch, I can feel the turmoil he's in. The pain and sense of betrayal. And I know I can't do anything to help him right now.

"We must hurry. I'm not the only one who knows of these passages," he says.

AJ looks back from where we came, her eyes shooting daggers at our newest enemies, but in rare style, she doesn't say anything. She can sense this isn't the time for the standard AJ sass.

The passage leads to a narrow stairwell that takes us down underneath the kingdom grounds. As we skulk through the passageway, trying our best to be fast but stealth, I reach out to Zev with my mind. *Where are you?*

But he doesn't reply.

I pray with all my soul that they didn't go wolf hunting while this double-cross was happening.

I know Revia was against the alliance, but I never could have fathomed something like this. This is Shakespearian-level villainy. Maybe Rune, when things are calmed down and he feels like talking about it, will have some insights into how everything went so horribly wrong.

For now, we just need to get out of this kingdom.

Rune silently guides us through the dusty, cramped, spider web covered stone halls and down a second long stairway, then out an inconspicuous wooden door, where we find ourselves standing on an underground dock, a wooden boat bobbing in the waters, tugging at the rope that moors it.

"The river is the fastest way past the kingdom walls and it flows toward Wiceraweil. That's where we need to get to right now."

"I can be of some use there," a voice growls, stepping out of the shadows. Zev walks over to us and pulls me into a fierce hug. "I'm sorry I couldn't answer you," he says, kissing my forehead and stepping back to address us all. "I came running when I heard commotion, and I was with Erzsébet before."

I open my mouth to speak but he beats me to it. "Rain is happy, healthy, and safe. And I think having a baby to care for has done Erzsébet a lot of good."

I snap my mouth shut, relief pouring into me at his words.

Unfortunately, I sense a big but, and he's right on time to deliver it.

"But there is some bad news too. I'll explain when we're on the river."

As we are boarding the boat, we hear shouting coming from the passage we just left.

I hold up my wand to do something about it when AJ shakes her head, then closes her eyes. She reaches a hand over the side of the boat so her fingers graze the water's surface. For a moment nothing happens. Then everything happens.

Water pours from the river and begins to circle around itself, forming a huge ball. Once it's positioned in front of the door we just walked through, it freezes into a giant boulder.

"Let them try to get through that," she mutters, a gleam of pride showing in her eyes. I stare at the massive ball of ice, my mouth hanging open. She's really taking to her powers, and I'm impressed.

Once we're all in, AJ gives the water a nudge and we make fast time down the river. The mountain is still giving us shelter for a time, but eventually, we'll pop out into the open world. Hopefully, they'll have lost our trail by then.

As Rune navigates the boat and AJ manipulates the water, I fill Zev in on what happened. I do it mentally so Rune doesn't have to rehash his parent's murder.

This is devastating, Zev says when I've finished. *For Rune and for all of us. We would have had an easier time convincing the wolves to join us had we already aligned the other two kingdoms.*

"I know," I whisper out loud, squeezing his hand.

AJ continues magically propelling us downstream, towards the werewolf kingdom. After a moment of silence, I remember Zev had some news to deliver.

"So where were you? Why didn't you bring back my baby? And what did Erzsébet tell you that's so terrible? And also, why didn't you bring back my baby?" I need my damn baby.

"The witch queen intercepted a message sent by crow with the *Érintett* plans. She didn't know who it was intended for, but the use of hidden ink made her believe it came from Timót." Zev's nostrils flare before he continues. "He's poised to attack Wiceraweil during the Blood Moon. In three nights. It's a mating time for dragons, meaning they'll be particularly... aggressive."

"But didn't we just have a full moon?" I ask. "That was the whole reason you had to shift."

"In our world the full moon lasts longer. A full seven-day cycle every month, with each day carrying a different significance."

"That's not enough time," I say, my pitch and volume rising with my agitation. "We lost the fae, who might even be working against us at this point. The vampires are only on our side because half of them are dead and the rest are scared. And the wolves..." I look away from Zev, reluctant to finish my sentence.

"I know, love," he says. "That's why we must hurry. The werewolves, vampires and two powerful witches will have to be enough. And I'll do whatever it takes to get the wolves on our side. Especially knowing that's where the dragons are headed."

Ugh. Why is shit so hard all the damn time?

I sound like a whiny toddler, even to myself, but I'm really over all this. I just want my baby, and my bar, and maybe a piano. That's it. That's the perfect life.

But then I glance at Rune, his aristocratic profile, his kind eyes, and I think of all he's given up to help me. And I look to Zev, whose gaze searches the distance, towards his homeland, but whose heart, I can feel, is diving deep into the past. And I think of Darius, enduring unimaginable torture to hold together this fragile alliance.

And I know.

I can't give them up for an easier life. I won't.

Sometimes it's the hardest paths, the steepest hills, that provide the greatest reward.

Life isn't meant to be easy. It's meant to shape us into someone capable of handling the hard times.

My poor baby is gonna be the toughest kid in town.

I shake my head, tearing myself away from my

thoughts, and take in the scenery around me as we float down the underground river. We've come to the base of a slope and Rune now pulls on a massive rope, guiding our boat up a watery incline. AJ sits at the back of the vessel, magically prompting the water to help push us along. After a minute or so, we emerge through a small cave leading from under the fae kingdom and into the main river channel. Rune sits down, his first moment of stillness since we ran.

I inch closer to the fae and take his arm in mine, leaning my head against his shoulder.

I open my mouth but really don't have anything to say. No words can help in a situation like this.

He shakes his head slowly, a single tear trickling down his cheek. "My sister and I have always had our differences, but I never imagined…" He pauses, his voice catching. "I never imagined she'd be capable of this."

For a hot second I wondered if someone else did the murdering and Revia just assumed it was us, but Rune's instincts confirm my own.

That bitch.

Zev joins us, holding Rune from the other side. The two press their foreheads together, and I squeeze the tears out of my eyes seeing the affection between them. I hate that it took war, death, and a cruel prophecy to bring these three men back to one another, but I can't argue against the end result. They are closer than brothers. Closer than lovers in many ways. It's a bond that goes back lifetimes and shatters barriers. They have loved and lost and suffered together.

For her part, AJ has been unusually quiet. She's sitting on the edge of the boat in mermaid form, letting her tail dangle in the water as she uses her fin to guide us. But her real focus is on her pendant. Leo.

After all these years, it looks like we've both finally found our type: not human.

We pass the rest of the journey in silence, Zev and I offering what comfort we can to Rune, who continues his long stare into the distance. He has many human lifetimes of memories to reflect on right now, and a boat ride to another kingdom won't be nearly enough time to process all that, but at least it's a start.

I GET a sense we're almost there when the sun starts to rise and I notice a change in topography. The type of tree is different, and mountains loom in the distance. Not the snowy peaked ones that cut down the middle of this world, but the green, lush mountains surrounded by the shimmering blue waters that look just as magical here as they do in the fae land.

I can also feel that we're getting closer by how Zev's energy shifts. I'm always connected to my mate, but the closer we are physically, the stronger that connection is. He's nervous about being home, and I don't blame him one bit.

If this whole adventure has taught me anything it's that homecomings are fraught with drama. Holy hell.

We hear wolves howling in the distance, and I'm startled when Zev begins to join in. Though he doesn't shift, what comes from his throat is more beast than man.

"They know we're here," Zev says, when the howling dies down.

"No shit, Sherlock," AJ says, twisting to face him. "You just announced our presence."

Zev rolls his eyes at my salty friend. "I responded because they knew already and were going to attack. Now we will have an escort instead."

AJ snorts. "Escorts. Guards. Sounds like the same thing to me."

I can't disagree with her, so I just shrug. "What now?"

Zev lifts his chin to indicate a bridge in the distance. "Dock there. They will meet us and escort us to the king and queen."

I stifle a yawn as AJ begins to guide our bow to its destination.

When we disembark, a dozen wolves surround us, teeth bared, snarling. Zev instantly shifts and nips at a few of them, putting them in their place. They all submit, whining and creeping back, offering their necks. It's clear Zev is asserting his dominance as an alpha and prince, but God it's such a pissing contest it's hard to take too seriously.

The only wolf that doesn't shrink back much is a large gray one in the front. The gray wolf shifts and Zev does the same. The two men have similarities: their body shape and hair color mainly, but where Zev is much taller and exudes alpha energy, the other man is definitely a beta who wishes he was an alpha. It sours his looks, and his whole vibe. I instantly know A; this is Zev's brother and B; this guy gives me the sceevies.

Zev reaches for my hand, and I join him, clutching his arm and trying not to act like I'm scared of being surrounded by wolves. "Alden, this is

Bernadette, the mother of the Last Witch, and my mate."

The wolves scrape the ground in agitation and Alden raises an eyebrow. "Mate? That's...unexpected."

AJ clears her throat, clearly annoyed at being ignored.

"And her friend, AJ," Zev says with an amused grin.

AJ gets Alden's attention, that's for sure. Little does he know he's in competition with a ghost.

"Bernie, this is my brother Alden."

I hold out a hand to shake his, but he ignores it and I drop mine, my cheeks burning in embarrassment but also anger that he's being a dick.

So far, the only family members of my guys who have been pleasant are dead.

"Mother's waiting," Alden says turning on his heels.

We've only taken a few steps away from the water and towards the hill leading up the mountain when the wolves freak the hell out.

That's when I hear it. The voice a gentle breeze against my mind.

"Darius!" I scream his name, tears blurring my vision as I search for him.

He's by my side in a flash, and Zev has to puff out

his chest to get the other wolves to settle themselves as Darius pulls me into a hard embrace.

As our flesh touches, our souls connect once again, and the piece of me that's been emptied out is refilled with painfully sharp reminders of his torment. When we finally push our bodies apart, I study his face. He looks... different. His eyes are darker, his face narrower. I run my fingers through a streak of silver hair that wasn't there before. "I thought you had another day," I ask softly.

He shakes his head. *My brother freed me after the second night. As a show of good faith.*

There's an agony in his voice that shakes me to the core. Even serving two-thirds of his sentence, he just sat alone in the darkness for two thousand years. I pull him closer to me, trying to transfer my lifeforce to him.

Zev's brother sneers. "I thought she was *your* mate? Not some bloodsucker's whore."

That was exactly the wrong thing to say right now.

Zev, Darius, and even Rune, who's been mostly checked out, come together as one to offer an incredibly menacing and threatening display that sends Alden stumbling back and mumbling something incomprehensible.

I'm not sure that won't come back to bite us in the ass later, but either way I'm grateful we're all together again.

Except my damn baby. I need Rain so much it hurts. That witch better not let a hair on my precious girl get touched or I'll never forgive myself.

As much as I know she shouldn't be here, it's still so hard to be away from her. I guess this is what it's like as a working mom. Though my work is decidedly a bit unique.

"Let's press on before the sun brings full daybreak," Zev says with a wink to Darius. Alden growls at the show of affection to the vampire then begrudgingly leads us all forward.

I try very hard to keep my mind from mentally slamming Darius with word vomit, but I can't help but ask at least one question. *Are you okay?*

He glances over at me. He still hasn't let go of my hand. *I will be.*

His dark eyes pierce into me, and I promise him that as soon as we have a minute, he needs to feed on me. I can tell he hasn't had blood since last I saw him and it's not having a great effect on his general health.

We enter the werewolf kingdom through a mountain tunnel that looks like it's for trains... but that's because I have a dumb human brain. As soon as we pass through the threshold, the tunnel walls give way to a massive, underground city, with stone streets passing between clay buildings. It's the secret village every kid dreams of constructing in a mound of dirt, just a billion times more extravagant. Lighting columns along the street look like they filter sunlight from the mountain down to underground luminaires, though right now everything is lit with fire pits and candles. It's rustic and futuristic all at once.

Our handlers, or whatever the wolves escorting us are called, lead us along the roads to an unbelievable palace at the center of the city. Marble cylinders stand in front of the entryway, with gold patterns decorating the entire structure. I keep worrying that an earthquake will bring the mountain crumbling down and destroy all this beauty, but then I remind myself that this city has clearly been here a long time and won't be going anywhere anytime soon.

We are escorted down a hallway and through enormous double doors made of oak and elaborately carved. I know that we'll meet the king and queen of the werewolves on the other side of this door, and they just so happen to be the parents of my werewolf mate. My nerves start to spike as we walk in and turn towards the thrones.

Except there's only his mother, not his father. That takes some of the pressure off, but it also feels odd. The queen sits on her throne with a sad expression on her aged yet timeless face. Her eyes are the same green as Zev's, but her hair is lighter, grayed by time.

Zev lowers himself to a knee, though he keeps his eyes on his mother with a confused expression in his eyes.

"Rise my son. We need not stand on ceremony. Not when times such as these are upon us," the queen says.

Zev stands and approaches his mother, taking her hand. "Where is Father?"

The queen shakes her head. "Your father is sick. We hoped you'd come back in time, and I wish I could greet you in higher spirits."

"A new war is coming," Zev says. "We need the wolves. How ill is he, and for how long?"

She frowns. "He's gone to Mount Arys. He's said his farewells."

She turns away from Zev, looking now at the empty chair beside her.

"We cannot help you. Not when we are about to lose our king."

CHAPTER FOURTEEN

Things just keep going from bad to worse with family affairs. I reach for Zev's hand instinctively, as worry and tension radiate off of him.

His mother raises an eyebrow in surprise. She sniffs the air, making me super self-conscious about BO, then frowns. "You've mated. With a *witch*."

She doesn't even bother trying to hide her condescension.

Zev pulls me closer to him. "Yes. Mother, this is Bernadette, my mate."

The queen ignores me as her gaze lands on first Rune then Darius. "And you've brought our enemies with you as well, I see."

This time her tone is harder to read, but she's for sure not happy about any of this. Then again, her husband is dying. She's probably not happy about anything.

"He is unfit to lead," Alden says bluntly, turning his mother's attention to himself. "He consorts with the enemy, and not only is his mate a witch, she's already mated to a vampire and fae."

The queen's eyes are sharp when she turns them on Zev. "Is this true?"

Zev squeezes my hand, assuring me the queen's judgment means nothing. "Bernie is a powerful witch, more powerful than any we have ever known. Through hardship and oath, she has formed a bond with all three of us. But we chose to bind ourselves to her. And whether she's a wolf or not, my wolf chose her. You know that is unbreakable, in life or death." He growls at the end, his alpha energy consuming the room.

His mother waves him off. "None of this matters while our king faces the end of his life."

"What happened to him?" Zev asks.

His brother answers. "Magic is dying. He took a tusk during a hunt, and now he cannot heal or shift back. The wound is festering, killing him slowly. You were meant to bring back the prophesied child who would save us, not mate with the mother and destroy your kind in the process."

He throws each word like a dagger at Zev, who remains stoic in face of the verbal wounds.

I'm done with this bullshit, and I do not remain so stoic. "Listen, shithead. That's my daughter you're talking about. Killing my baby won't fix your magical drought, and you all need to really start thinking more creatively if you don't want to go the way of the DoDo birds. The Last Witch will not die in your kingdom. And if you help us, she might not even be the *Last* Witch."

Alden, who I can tell really loves being called out by a non-wolf female, nearly shifts in front of us and looks ready to tear out my throat. Zev steps forward, his eyes glowing as he growls at his brother. "Do not lay a hand on her."

"Stop this, both of you," the queen says, standing. "Someone will show you to your rooms. Do as you please tonight, tomorrow we will talk about this… situation," she says, her eyes flinching at Zev's penetrating look. Then she turns and storms out.

Alden hisses at me, then turns to follow her, and one of the other guards steps forward awkwardly. "I guess follow me?"

We follow the guard through the palace. It seems like Zev is being treated as a stranger in his home land and I can't tell if that's custom or my fault. If I had to guess, I'd say I'm the problem. Or really, our whole entourage is.

I'm intrigued by every bit of architecture in the city. Floating down the river, I didn't know what to expect. Do werewolves live in caves? Penthouses? Tree forts? My mind put in plenty of hours trying to envision what this land might look like, but it was always filtered through my limited human perceptions. At some point I'll have to learn not to listen to that part of my brain.

Turns out, it's sort of a mix of all of it. Our suite features exquisite natural materials, with stone walls polished until they gleam a deep smokey gray with flecks of sparkling quartz, floors covered in hand woven carpets of earthy colors, overstuffed furniture for lounging before the fire, and bedrooms for all of us. They guys choose to stay in the rooms closest to me, while AJ takes the furthest one away.

"I need some alone time," she says softly, one hand on her pendant.

I purse my lips, worried about my bestie, but then nod. "Sure. Get some rest. It's been a long day."

She snorts at that and closes her door behind her firmly. A few moments later I hear her talking to her ghost.

I take a quick pass through my room, charmed by the decor but feeling like I can't really enjoy it.

My closet comes stocked with a few fancy garments, and though I don't much feel like dressing up, I'm grateful to be able to get out of the dirty clothes I've been wearing. I change into a periwinkle dress, kicking my tattered fae clothing into the back corner of the closet.

I head to the common area, looking prettier than I feel. Zev won't stop pacing the room, even when a meal of venison and roasted vegetables are delivered.

"You should eat something," I plead.

Rune usually helps in these situations, but he shuffled off to his room for some well-earned wallowing.

And Darius has been withdrawn since he returned from his torture, which I definitely don't blame him for. I can't even imagine what he's processing.

My poor guys have lost so much.

Zev ignores my pleas to eat, and I set the plate down, unable to muster up much of an appetite for myself either.

Zev's wolf is close to the surface, making the man edgy and anxious.

I cross the room to take his hand, my worry for

him creasing my brow. "If you want to go spend some time with your mother, we'll keep ourselves busy."

He stops pacing to face me, his forest green eyes full of unexpressed emotion. My beautiful werewolf has only been back in his kingdom for a few hours and already seems different. He's more distant, more serious than usual. But through our bond I can feel the truth. He's scared. He's scared of his father dying, or not dying but staying incapacated. He's scared of what's coming and what will happen to his people.

I feel all this through our bond as I offer what comfort I can.

"There's nothing to be done," he says gruffly as he pulls me into his muscular arms, sliding his hands around my hips. "If a wolf knows they're dying, they leave for Mount Arys to go in peace. My father, and all his subjects, are simply waiting for death."

The words sound hollow coming from his lips.

"Are you going to go see him?" I study his face to try and read him, but his heart speaks to me more powerfully. Grief rises in him like a wave, coming from the depths of his past, an old pain that has never healed.

He nods, his eyes glossy with emotion. "It's not customary to visit the still living at Mount Arys, but… the news of this has shaken me. I had no idea how bad things had gotten..." he drifts off, and I see in his eyes he's trying to make sense of this. He had a plan. To convince his father to join us, or challenge him to a duel. But how can you duel a dying man?

After a moment he shakes his head to refocus. "If he was as he used to be, things would be different. Now, I don't know what to do."

"I'm sorry," I say softly. "I feel like getting people on our side shouldn't be this hard."

"Nothing is as it should be in the world right now," he says, his jaw tensing as he speaks. "The magical imbalance destroying us will eventually be felt in all realms. Even yours."

I think of my little Irish pub on the outskirts of Rowley and wonder what that would mean for my small town. Up to this point, every person I know is blissfully unaware of magic, the feuding realms, and certainly the fact that I'm a witch. They think I'm on vacation--not in a werewolf palace.

It's something we've talked about before, but the reality has never felt so immediate as it does now. Sure, we've been attacked, and I've nearly died more times than I can count since meeting the three Sexies. But being here, in the different kingdoms of my men, I realize more than ever what the stakes are for all of them. And though I'll always put the well being of

223

my baby above everything else--even if that means being away from her for days--I finally understand the desperation all of the kingdoms are dealing with.

They want to save their people from extinction.

And if they'll let me, I'm going to try to help.

Before I can dwell on these big-picture issues, we need to defeat Timót and his army. Aside from a squadron of dragons, I don't know exactly how many fight in his ranks. After the showdown in Vaemor, I feel very confident we need more than just the vampires on our side. The fae blew it, and now things are off to a rocky start with the wolves.

Kings and queens have been picking really shitty times to die.

Zev looks at the floor, battling his emotions. I lift his chin so our eyes meet, then pull him closer and seek out his lips.

The kiss starts tenderly. A kiss of shared pain, shared love, shared sorrow and shared joy.

But as we lose ourselves in each other, the kiss changes to something passionate and deep. It holds within it all the swirling complexity of emotions we are both feeling. I feel our bond more profoundly when we are intimate, and the power of it swells up in me, merging with my own magic, creating a euphoria that's almost addictive.

A soft hiss from behind me interrupts our kiss, and I turn in Zev's arms to see Darius walking over. The vampire studies me with his obsidian eyes, consuming me with just a look.

"I need you," Darius says, his gaze locking on mine. He flashes to my side with his vampire swiftness, and I find myself pinned between him and Zev in the most delicious possible way. Two sets of hands has my skin begging for the dress to be removed.

I lean against Zev's chest as Darius presses into me, and the feel of them both ignites a deep, burning need in me that only my lovers can satiate.

Darius leans in, his teeth sharpening as he studies the vein in my neck. I sigh as he begins to drink from me. Though I no longer need him to feed from me for survival, the act remains incredibly intimate and powerful. And I know he needs not just my blood, but me, my essence, to heal the cracks that his centuries of confinement created.

Zev's body responds to the moment and I feel his hardness pressing against my back just as Rune steps out of the bedroom for the first time since we got here. He stares for a moment, then walks over to us. Darius pulls away from my neck and takes a step to the side, making room for the sexy fae who can't pull his eyes from the three of us.

My sweet, heart-heavy fae had only just opened himself to love again, and now I'm worried about how his horrible loss might affect him. I pull his face to mine, our noses and foreheads touching.

His silver eyes still hold the pain of loss and betrayal, but there's also a gleam of desire as well. It gives me hope that all three of them seem to take comfort in not just being with me, but being with each other as well.

As Rune's lips land on mine, Darius and Zev stroke my body into a heightened sense of arousal, and I feel all three of them in my soul, mixing with my magic, with my breath, with my very essence. I close my eyes, letting their hands, mouths and bodies blur into one orgasmic experience.

Zev's teeth are on my neck, scraping at the now healed flesh where Darius just fed. Rune continues to explore my mouth, nipping at my lower lip as he cups my face with his hands, and Darius is using one hand to tease at the hot, pulsing need between my legs, pressing through my gown, while his thumb rubs against my hardened nipples through the silk and satin.

Nothing has ever felt more right than having all three of my lovers with me like this, and I'm desperate to tear off all our clothes and find out what more we can do together, but just as I'm about to send buttons flying through the room, there's a knock at our door following the creaking sound of it opening.

Flushed and slightly embarrassed, I pull away from my men and adjust my dress as a servant comes in. She looks middle-aged, with some graying streaks in her dark hair, though for a werewolf that likely means she's very, very, very old, given how slowly I've heard they age.

"The queen has sent this for you, Your Highness," she says in a subservient voice, not looking directly at Zev but bowing in his general direction. Zev frowns, and the sexual tension we were all floating in just moments ago dissipates quickly with the reminder of why we're here.

He accepts the parchment from her and nods. "Thank you, Ally."

Ally bows again, glances my way quickly, then shirks back when we make eye contact. With mumbled apologies she quickly exits the room, leaving us alone once again.

I straighten my spine, trying to stay strong for whatever the night brings. But I know the guys can feel the nervous wave of energy threatening to consume me.

Rune takes my hand, and for the first time since his parent's death, his calming magic flows into me, soothing my unsettled mind.

"Thank you," I say with a smile. "You might want to give Zev some of that."

Zev just huffs in response and continues reading.

Darius approaches me from behind, dropping his lips to my neck seductively. *I would rather continue what we started than deal with anymore wolves.*

I turn to face the vampire, smirking at him. *Would that we could,* I say back to his mind. *But we should follow Zev's lead.*

Putting action to my words, I take Zev's hand and squeeze it. "What does it say?"

Zev looks up from the letter, his face a few shades paler. "It's from my mother. She…"

He walks over and drops the letter in the fireplace, watching it burn. "She's worried my brother will try to kill my father and become king. She wants me to stop him."

THE FOUR OF us make all haste in heading to Mount Arys, not knowing what we'll find when we get there.

We are silent as we hike through the woods, Darius keeping to the shadows to avoid the late afternoon sun. Zev suggested he stay back, but the vampire made it clear he's had enough alone time and would rather risk catching on fire than spend another moment with just his thoughts.

It's a tense hike for me. This isn't how any girl dreams of meeting her lover's dad, and I'm a little worried my presence might be the thing that actually kills him. Not only am I a poor bartender from New England who's 100% not a werewolf, I'm also bonded to a vampire and a fae--the two races this king has been at war with for centuries. I'm like the least ideal mate for the future werewolf king.

I shut out the uncomfortable thoughts by looking at my mate, trying to give him strength through my loving gaze. He doesn't look back, but I know he feels me.

I have a lot of questions about Alden. Is he really thinking of killing his father, or is the queen just trying to stir shit up? He seems like a dirtbag, but that could just be the magical imbalance destroying his realm that's affecting his mood.

Probably a combination of both.

As we reach the opening to a cave deep in the woods, Zev sprints off without a word. I'm confused for a second, then I hear the mournful howls of a dying wolf that had already caught his ears.

Darius has rejoined me and Rune beneath the shade of the trees, and we approach the entrance with a bit more caution. This is not a mountain we will be welcome inside.

When we reach the mouth to the cave, we hear the growling. It's not the sound of one wolf growling through pain, but three animals showing aggression. I pull out my wand, Darius pulls out his teeth, and Rune draws his sword as we follow. We find two wolves attacking each other; a large gray wolf lying on the ground covered in blood, one wound clearly fresher than the rest.

Rune runs over to the king and tries to work his healing magic on him. I aim my wand as Zev and his brother go at it, but I can't get a clean shot with the two constantly biting at each other's necks. Finally, when there's a bit of separation, I send a jolting shot into the gray wolf's chest that knocks him back. He's not seriously injured, but the way he whines you'd think I'd just shot off his balls.

When Darius steps forward, his elongated teeth on full display, brother dearest seems to realize he's way outmatched and runs away, dodging us as he leaves the cave and heads home with his tail between his legs.

Zev shifts to human form and runs to his father,

bending over his near-lifeless body as the king slowly shifts back from beast to man.

I wait for a Hallmark kind of death, where father and son say their last goodbyes and make amends. Where Zev's dad gives his blessing for his son to lead and bring peace to their people.

None of that happens.

The king never opens his eyes again.

With his last exhale, all is silent.

Zev looks far more angry than sad. He's lost his father, but his need to protect this new family carries more weight. He stands and turns toward the exit, murder in his eyes as he thinks of what his brother's just done.

"Zev..." I say, not knowing what he plans but thinking a little reflection might be useful before he acts. He doesn't seem to share my assessment.

"He'll try to rally the wolves," Zev says. "He may already be trying to kill our mother. If we..."

He stops talking, cocking his head to the side so he can listen. I can't hear a thing, but Zev's got wolf ears that put mine to shame.

Then I hear it. It starts softly before becoming unmistakable.

The sound of large, beating wings.

We run out of the cave and look up through the trees, my heart dropping in my chest at the site.

The evening sky is filled with dragons, circling around the wolves' mountain stronghold.

"I thought we had more time," I breathe, terror gripping me.

"We don't," Darius says.

The new war has begun.

CHAPTER FIFTEEN

Dragons descend from every direction, sheets of fire coating the hillsides and mountaintops. There's not a lot of excess foliage to burn, but the heat of the dragons' flames is so intense it doesn't need much fuel.

And we're running straight towards it.

Zev runs ahead as a wolf while I ride on the speedy Darius' back, sprinting with incredible speed and grace while avoiding even a flicker of sunlight. I'm not sure what the plan is, other than to face an impossibly strong army head-on. I race through different spells in my mind, but each feels like throwing an ice cube at a house fire. I'm not ready for this.

Scores of dragons flutter above the mountain,

each with a handful of fighters on its back. They breathe fire mercilessly, and I'm starting to think Timót's plan is to melt the entire werewolf kingdom. Which will be a real drag, because we're heading inside.

The dragons have their focus on the mountain, so passing under them isn't too difficult, though the flames feel way too close.

I'm drenched with sweat in seconds, which is how long it takes us to get inside the tunnel to the main city. There's a brief sense of relief at not being out in the open anymore, but that's quickly erased by the panic coming from being trapped inside a mountain.

Zev disappears into the city streets, maybe looking for his mother, maybe still planning to find and kill his brother. I'm not going to bother trying to have a mental conversation with him at this juncture.

Darius and Rune stay right by my side, neither with a plan beyond sacrificing themselves to save me.

We move further into the center of the city and away from the main entrances. I'm starting to wonder if this is the first time anyone has ever attacked the wolves and they have no plan to counter, but Darius steps into my mind and shoots that thought down, reminding me that all the races in this realm have been at war for hundreds of years.

"Where do we go?" I ask, not particular about who gives me an answer.

"Into the city center, then we wait for Zev to find us," Rune says. "No reason to come up with a plan other than whatever he thinks is best."

I appreciate the deference to the wolf prince, but since Zev isn't standing with us right now and I can see dragon fire sneaking through the entrances, I'd love to hear some additional ideas.

At that moment, every structure in the city bursts to life. Wolves leap and scramble through doorways and windows, climbing up narrow paths along the inside face of the mountain. None of them heads for the main tunnels, but instead climbs to smaller coves along the gigantic mountain walls.

Clearly, they have a plan.

Distracted as I am by the sight of the wolves in action, I turn immediately when Zev comes to my side and shifts back into human form. He's followed by AJ, which almost makes my heart burst. The world is chaos and death feels eminent, but my wolf still went to find my friend and make sure she was safe. There's no time for me to hug and kiss and thank him, so I just welcome as much of his spirit into me as I can while his body's close.

"We have tactical positions to assume," he says,

"but a thinned army of wolves is no match for dragons. I can't imagine we'll fare better than the vampires."

"Can we run?" I ask, with AJ nodding at the idea. There's not enough water for her to play with here, so she'd clearly rather be on the move.

"There are passages beneath the mountain that fan out to the headlands, but they're too narrow to fit a large group. Besides, most wolves would bark at the idea of leav--"

Zev's sentence is cut short when an arrow whips through the air behind us and strikes him in the shoulder, the impact taking him off his feet and slamming him against a nearby wall. Darius flashes over to help Zev as I turn to see where the attack came from.

Revia.

She and another twenty fae stand just inside the entrance on the opposite side of the mountain.

We've got dragons to our left, fae warriors to our right, and nowhere to go.

Rune has his sword drawn, standing his ground. Zev has morphed back into a wolf, the fur on his left front leg damp with blood, but the arrow is out in Darius' hand.

"We will kill you before you can kill us," Revia yells at her brother, another arrow drawn in her bow.

"How did our parents raise only one of us to be so dense?" Rune yells back, then swings his sword with incredible precision to deflect the arrow shot in response to his words. "We're trying to help all the races! We're trying to undo what's been done. Your actions only ensure more will die."

"You're blind, brother." Revia loads another arrow as the fae behind her begin fending off a few wolf attackers. She's got enough of an infantry to keep her safe while still having another ten guards stay focused on us. Meanwhile, the goddamn mountain around us is on fire.

"You've been led astray by the very subject of the prophecy," she says, slowly advancing towards us. "I've met this Timót you seem to fear so much. In fact, I sent him word right after your escape. He wants to save the fae from the vampires, then have the wolves bow to us as they were meant to. With him as our ally, the Last Witch--alive or dead--will bring magic back to our woods." She takes a break from her speech to fire another arrow, which again Rune strikes away. "If your pledges hadn't made you so disloyal, you'd understand."

Rune's teeth grind. "Interesting talk of loyalty from someone who just killed her own parents, the rulers of the kingdom she claims to love so fiercely."

His words strike a chord, as Revia's face scrunches in reaction, but she shakes it off and dives back into her self-deluded narrative. "Leadership comes with a price," she says.

She plucks another arrow, but an enormous rumble makes everyone freeze. The entire city shakes and all of the buildings sway. From the mountain walls above the far entrance, hundreds of wolves run back inside, many with their fur singed and smoking. There's a momentary lull...

And then the mountain wall explodes.

Dirt flies in every direction as a cacophonous mixture of crashing debris and howling wolves fills the air. Before I know what's happening, Darius has lifted both me and Zev and rushed us around the corner of a building for shelter.

When he sets me down, I peer out and look for Rune. The air is thick with dust, but I see his profile standing right where he was, still facing off against his sister. I get the feeling they'll both try to ignore the dragons in favor of settling this very personal score.

As visibility returns, I can see daylight coming through the massive hole leading into the outside world. Zev now stands in human form over my shoulder, his rage almost bubbling over as he takes in the damage. Seems like the dragons weren't trying to melt the whole mountain, only soften it enough to break through.

"These mountain walls have withstood every attack since my great grandfather claimed this land," Zev says in a shaky voice. "Those dragons will pay."

Darius puts a hand on his friend's non-wounded shoulder. "Let's start with the man who controls the dragons. It's his head we want."

I expect to see a burst of fire or a massive reptilian head slink through the opening, and hold my breath while waiting for what's to come. A quick glance at the fae soldiers shows they're waiting as well, though they all look pretty calm.

The army we hoped to align with has allegiance with our enemy.

God I hate Rune's sister.

When there's finally movement along the exploded wall, I ready my wand to cast some sort of shield, though I don't know if any spell can protect us from dragon breath.

Instead of a dragon, however, I see men. Timót's soldiers.

They come in by the dozens, using the walkways the wolves took to come down to the ground floor. When we flew into Vaemor, Timót had maybe fifty men; now there are hundreds. It's a larger sampling of the different races I saw before, with orcs walking alongside humans alongside shifters and dwarves. They march in, firing arrows or shooting spells at any wolf that dares approach.

I'd almost rather face off against the dragons than this army of creeps.

Even though it's a long way to the opening in the mountain wall, I still recognize my father when he steps into rubble, backlit by the sun and looking as powerful as he thinks he is.

I want nothing more than to take him down a peg.

Behind him, his enormous dragon flaps its wings, hovering outside the entrance. It'll be a tight squeeze, but I'm not about to bet that thing can't make its way inside the city. Looks like I might get to face off against these shitty soldiers *and* a dragon.

Timót barks orders at his troops, but he's too far away for me to hear. If I had to guess, I'd say he's telling them not to kill me or the baby. Even though Rain isn't here, just the idea of her is making our attackers approach with caution. We'll see how much we can use that to our benefit.

I'm shocked when Rune appears beside me, as I can still see him standing in the open street facing his sister. My brain knows he's created an illusion, but my eyes don't trust my brain at all. The fae sees Zev's wound and sets to healing it while the army continues descending into the city. We're not well hidden, but we're not in a direct sight line. As the *Érintett* fighters get closer, I can hear some of their calls--"bring out the witch and the city lives," and "deliver the Last Witch or face the dragons."

We're huddled against a wall, trapped in a mountain. Hiding won't save us.

I'm about to stand, to offer myself up, when Darius grabs my arm to keep me still.

Don't you dare, he says.

It's the only way. Timót won't kill me.

You don't know that.

Our conversation is interrupted by a loud crash that answers my question about the size of the opening in the wall--Timót, on the back of his massive dragon, has landed on the city floor not too far from Rune's illusory self. He's covered in a shimmering cloak from head to toe, one that looks like iridescent chainmail. There's a matching helmet that leaves a small slit for his eyes and mouth.

Dragon armor, Darius says in my mind. *To protect him from the sun.*

Oh shit. I completely forget that my disgusting dad was also a vampire. And apparently one who scaled a dragon so he could still enjoy the daytime. What a prick.

Revia fires an arrow, not at Timót since apparently they're great friends, but at what she believes is her brother. It passes through his pretend body and dissipates the illusion.

"Where are they?" Timót asks.

"Near," the fae princess answers. "Though they don't have the child."

"What?" My father sounds angry. He's kept his cool through horrifying situations, and that was before he became immortal, so his rage is extra unsettling.

"They escaped Aevelairith by boat, the witch queen has the baby--"

"You didn't make that clear in your missive," Timót seethes.

"What does it matter?" Revia fires back. "The child can be tracked later and returned to the fae to fulfill the prophecy. First we can capture or kill the others."

My wand is shaking with magical anxiety. This feels like an opportunity to bring down at least one enemy, but there are too many and I don't know where to start. I'm also a little curious to see where this argument is headed.

Peering around the fallen column of a building, I can see my father on top of his dragon, his wand at his side. He stares at Revia, calculating his next move.

"You don't quite understand my intention," Timót says. "The child has a greater, more important purpose within the *Érintett* kingdom."

"Your agreement was to help the fae," Revia says. "You swore an oath."

"I did. A living oath."

Oh shit. What a tricky bastard.

"And then I died."

Before Revia can make sense of what's just been said, Timót rears back on the reins at his dragon's neck and the beast sends a flurry of fire toward the fae army. Some are far enough away to run or dive to the side, evading the worst of the fire. Standing front and center, only yards away from the dragon's mouth, Revia becomes charcoal before she can move an inch.

That takes care of one of our problems, and yet I don't feel one iota safer.

The surviving fae lower their weapons, looking as sheepish as they should. Fooled by this sinister man into thinking he believed in their cause. Now they have the blood of the royals on their hands.

"Bring in the rest of the dragons," Timót bellows.

"Search the grounds for the witch's mother and keep her alive if you can. If we don't find her within the hour… burn the mountain to the ground."

I feel Zev's growl in my bones before I can hear it, and know he's about to go die a fiery death if I don't do something. I ignore Darius' pleas and Rune's effort to grab my arm, and step out from the crumbled wall that was concealing us.

"Dad, why can't you be less evil?"

I don't have a plan, but that's never stopped me from talking shit in the past. I only hope AJ doesn't join in, because last time it almost killed her. My princes rise to stand behind me, though none makes a move to draw me back or come between me and my father. They know better at this point.

Timót smiles at me, and he looks genuinely happy to see me. How broken his brain must be, that he wants me to stay alive and be part of the vile kingdom he's trying to create.

"My girl, I've been worried. You knocked me out for days with your spell in Vaemor, and I wondered if the vampires had killed you while I was incapacitated. I'm so glad you're alright."

As he speaks, dragon after dragon crawls through the devastated mountain wall. Big as this underground city felt when we first arrived, the introduction of multiple dragons makes it feel much smaller.

A bright yellow dragon crawls toward us, a number of ogre-ish men on its back. There's anger in the monster's giant eyes, and I feel in my bones it has more to do with those riding it than the people it's approaching.

"Wherever have you left your child, Bernadette?" my father asks. "And how can you bring yourself to let the Last Witch out of your sight?"

"I don't know, dad, maybe it's because everyone's always trying to kill me and it's harder to point a wand with a baby on my tit."

Speaking with this wretched man really brings out the bartender in me. It's like talking with a belligerent drunk who's after my phone number, only worse in every conceivable way.

"I understand your feelings, but you must see the error in your choices." Timót gestures to the ravaged city around us, a shell of its former beautiful self. Wolf bodies are scattered around the grounds, while the living animals sit with their tails tucked, fearful of what will happen next. He's not wrong--destruction follows wherever I go.

"You can't have her, dad," I snap back, not ready to take the blame for the atrocities he's causing. "You can keep fighting and killing and destroying, and maybe one day you'll get your way, but then you can live alone in a shitty world surrounded only by the people who were shitty enough to be your followers."

I was just barfing out insults because I'm pissed, but this last line seems to have hit its mark. I can see the anger in Timót's eyes as he throws quick looks at the men in his command. They're a strange collection of angry and ornery, the type of guys who want to get in fights to distract from their other shortcomings. My dad's smarter than them, clearly, and wants to be better. But this is what his cause attracts. I see now that he wants to gain respect through his powers, and so far he's only respected by people he loathes.

The yellow dragon draws even closer. Should its riders pull the reins, me and my companions will meet a fiery death within seconds.

"You make this very difficult, Bernadette," Timót says, trying to keep his cool even as angry spittle flies out of his mouth. He starts to raise his wand, taking aim at me. I fight my fear, still believing he won't try to kill me, and trusting I have the speed and power to deflect a spell. I'm not really that scared, more curious to see what he'll try to do.

But I don't get a chance to find out.

A burst of light comes from the highest point

inside the mountain walls, and rocks and dirt come falling down as we all shield our faces. From a new opening in the underground castle, a glowing figure twirls down toward the city floor. No one makes a move; we're all too mesmerized by this dramatic entrance.

When she lands, I feel the most powerful sense of relief.

Accompanied by absolute terror.

Erzsébet.

And Rain.

She holds my baby in a neat little bundle, looking like the coolest grandma since Tilly. She smiles at me with her eyes before turning her focus to Timót.

"What a nice surprise," my awful dad says. "You've brought just what I needed."

"Oh, I'm dreadfully sorry, Timót," the witch responds. "The baby's not for you."

In the fanfare of Erzsébet's entrance, I missed the rest of the dragons crawling into the city. There are probably still more outside the mountain, but we're now completely surrounded, with twenty or more of the enormous creatures along the perimeter, all facing the witch queen and my child.

I really admire this woman, but her arrival was disastrously timed.

There's hot breath warming my shoulder, and I look briefly at the yellow dragon. It's the only one not focused on Erzsébet or Timót. Instead, its eyes are on me. That shouldn't come as a relief, but for some reason it does. I'm reminded of my moment with the dying mother in the cave, and finding peace in the creature's eyes. This dragon has the same look, even though peace should be the last thing on my mind.

"It's not too late to form an alliance, Erzsébet," Timót says. "When will you see that your plans for protecting the witches will never work?"

The queen stares back at him, a mix of pity and disgust on her face. "Blinded by power, young Timót. Just like so many who came before you. I'm sorry I couldn't offer better guidance. You've always been a clever man, and there was a better path for you to take."

Timót looks bored by the lecture and tries to move things along. "Give me the baby and save some lives. Perhaps even your own, depending on how I feel."

"Your threats don't carry much weight with an old woman like myself," Erzsébet says, slowly moving in my direction. "Bernadette, come to your baby. She's missed her mother."

I feel panic radiate off the Sexies behind me as I

step further out into the open. I keep my wand aimed at Timót, knowing an attack from him is the only thing I can fend off. I just have to trust the dragons aren't about to light us up. As I move, there's a gutteral noise that comes from the closest dragon. I don't speak it's language, but I'd swear it's calling to me.

Timót's angry glare bounces between Erzsébet and me, but he makes no move to act. The queen's right about his intelligence, and he knows he's currently outmatched magic-wise, plus he doesn't want to hurt the baby. What he'll do after the exchange remains to be seen.

It's so hard not to drop my wand and bring Rain in for a giant hug, but I manage as I take her into my left arm. The touch of my child almost brings me to my knees, but I stay strong for her. I keep my focus so I can keep her alive.

"Back away, dear," Erzsébet says to me, her eyes again locked on Timót. "I have to endure a quick duel with your father."

I do as she says, though I'm not excited about what this all means. One on one, I've got my money on the queen. One on one with the backing of a dragon army--I think we're all screwed.

"You've always thought your powers were enough,"

Timót says, keeping his wand trained on the queen as she strides gracefully over fallen stones toward the center of the city. "Your hubris has been the downfall of your kind, and now it will bring about your end."

Erzsébet reaches a platform and steps upon it, bringing herself closer to eye level with Timót, who's been turning on his dragon so he can keep the witch in his sights.

"I view it as a new beginning," the queen says.

I'd say my heart is racing, but I actually think it's stopped. I'm so racked with terror that my insides are paralyzed.

Timót stares a moment longer, then lifts his wand, aiming it not at Erzsébet but instead toward the hole in the mountain ceiling above. The witch queen holds her own wand in front of her, gripping it with two hands, waiting on her enemy's next move.

"*Támadás!*" Timót yells. Nothing happens with his wand, but I think the posture was just that-- posturing. The action comes from all around us.

In unison, every dragon rears its head back, then sends fire at the target. The heat is excruciating, even though I'm far from where the flames are headed. It burns my eyes, but I can't look away from Erzsébet. She's too smart, too strong, too powerful.

She's too important.

There's no way she can survive this onslaught of fire, but there's also no way she can die. I need her too much.

Rain needs her too much.

At first, the blaze encircles but doesn't touch her. There's a blue forcefield around the queen that keeps her from melting. Her eyes are closed and she looks relatively peaceful, though I'm sure her mind is super strained as she fights for control.

Slowly and with great purpose, she starts to lift her wand. My spirits perk up just a smidge, expecting she'll do something absolutely wild, like send all the flames back into the dragons' mouths and explode all of our enemies. She must have something cool like that up her sleeve.

Then she does something I don't understand--she turns her wand so the tip faces back toward her. She keeps both hands on the hilt, with the diamond point directed at her stomach.

Why?

In a sudden burst, the force field disappears, the flames engulf her--

And she plunges her wand into her gut.

She instantly disappears in the flames, a huge fire

column in her place, reaching all the way up to the opening at the top of the mountain.

She's dead.

She's gone.

Or is she?

High above where she stood, in the middle of the skyward flame, two giant wings fan out.

A mighty red bird hovers in the fire. Or perhaps it's part of the fire. The cry of a phoenix rings out through the underground city. While the dragons continue leveling their fiery breath at what was once the queen of the witches, the powerful wings repel the blaze back to the source. The dragons seem confused and flustered, and they keep scorching the center of the city where Erzsébet stood.

It's mayhem.

And it's given us our chance.

I spin to Rune, who knows my thoughts immediately, wiping his hands frantically to create an illusion.

Zev, I say in my mind, *get us the hell out of here.*

The words have barely left my thoughts when I feel teeth on my back.

But they're not vampire teeth. And they're not werewolf teeth.

Bigger.

Hotter.

Dragon teeth.

Aside from the burn, it doesn't really hurt. There's pressure from the grip, but it's not crushing my bones. I hold onto Rain with all my might, not bothering to aim my wand because I've got to make sure my baby doesn't fall.

I'm lifted into the air, swung around and genty thrown--right onto the back of the yellow dragon. For the briefest second, I'm face to face with a mean-looking orc, who's just as surprised to see me as I am to see him.

Just as he opens his mouth to scream, the dragon's teeth chomp down on him. This bite isn't nearly so gentle. The creature thrashes his body from side to side, and I listen to bones breaking while watching blood fly. The forceful shaking knocks the other men off the dragon's back, then the beast flings the now lifeless body to the ground.

"Grab on!" I yell to my friends.

The sense of peace I got from this dragon holds firm, and I know it's on our side. I don't know why, but I'm not about to doubt it. With four friends needing to join us and the dragon having four legs, I figure this is the perfect vehicle to get us out of here--until Darius speeds off in the other direction.

I open my mind to scream, but he speaks first. *I must travel in the tunnels and the shadows to avoid the sun. I will find you at Aevelairith, my love.*

Everyone else leaps to hold onto a leg just as the expansive wings start to flap. I look up to see if the rest of the army has turned on us, but most of the dragons are still breathing fire on the inflammable phoenix. The cylinder of fire still stretches between the floor and the roof high above.

While Timót's dragon continues its fire barrage, my father has turned his attention in our direction, confused by both the illusion and the yellow dragon that's broken ranks. He doesn't really see what's happening, so this is our chance.

"*Unar*," I say under my breath, though the intensity of my voice makes the spell as powerful as if I'd screamed it. A second later, Timót's wand flies out of his hand, clattering to the ground behind him.

One less threat. Now I just hope this young dragon is up to the task of outmaneuvering all its friends.

Another few beats of its wings and we're in the air, picking up momentum faster than I would have expected. I'm also surprised when our living transport heads upward and toward the center of the underground city as opposed to the larger opening in the side of the mountain.

We're going straight for the column of fire.

As we close in on the blaze, I see the head of the phoenix turn in our direction. It's like slow motion as we move closer and I stare at the bird, wondering if it's Erzsébet I'm seeing.

When we're only a few feeting from the cylinder of fire, the bird dives back toward the ground, bringing the flames down with it and washing the city floor in a blue fire. Now it's chaos below us--and freedom above.

I squeeze Rain tightly against my chest while holding the reins with my other hand. This ascent better not last much longer or gravity will get the best of me.

The other dragons have left the ground to get away from the fire spread at their feet, but they don't seem to care about us. The men on their backs don't know what to do without Timót shouting orders, and he's trying to gather his wand without getting burned.

As we near the top of the mountain, I look back to the flames below us. To the last spot I saw Erzsébet standing. Now it's just scorched ground and ash.

Our dragon bursts through the opening in the

mountaintop, continuing to fly higher. I keep my hold on the reins, finding a strength I didn't know I possessed to keep me and Rain alive. There are dragons flying around the outside of the mountain, as I thought there would be, but they're all lower than us. Before any makes a move, we're soaring well above them.

The dragon levels out, finally giving my arm a break, and continues flying through the clouds, never slowing down as it rushes us away from the danger.

I look down and breathe a sigh of relief. AJ, Zev and Rune are all safely holding on to the dragon's slender legs. I close my eyes and sense Darius moving beneath the earth, escaping the melay.

My family is safe.

Except for one.

CHAPTER SIXTEEN

The dragon flies through the clouds for a few more minutes, then ducks its mighty head and takes us back toward the ground. It keeps swerving and changing course, which is absolutely nauseating, but probably meant to keep any trackers off its path.

Frankly, I don't understand how this creature knows to be so helpful.

Is... is Erzsébet the dragon?

She's not, of course, because I saw her turn into fire as we escaped. That doesn't stop me from wanting to believe that she sent a part of herself into the dragon's mind so she could stay with us but in a different form.

I need to believe something like that. It makes it easier to understand what she did.

Tears blur my vision, and I don't have a hand to wipe them away. I just stare into space, wondering where--and if--this dragon will set us down.

The crunching of branches answers my question in short order as the magnificent yellow flyer breaks through a dense canopy of trees and lands with a jarring thud on the ground below. The choice was probably made to stay hidden from overhead, which is great; the scrapes and scratches endured by the people holding onto the dragon's legs are less appreciated.

She lowers her head, turning her long neck into a slide for me to climb down. I do so as gracefully as possible, and when my feet touch the ground, I finally have the chance to kiss and cuddle my sweet baby girl.

I feel like she's bigger, smarter, more alert since the last time I saw her. I missed so much in the last couple days and I'm about to mourn the lost time, when a calming touch from Rune reminds me that our distance probably kept Rain alive. Whether or not that's true, I'll just have to believe it so I don't hate myself too much.

"Where are we?" AJ asks, tending to a decent-sized cut on her forearm. "I need water before I go insane and try to fight this dragon."

I turn back to the majestic, gorgeous beast, sitting calmly with its head still on the ground. It seems so gentle now after causing such terror when it was part of an army helmed by shitbirds.

My companions stand a few yards away, not quite as trusting of the creature as I am. I don't blame them; it certainly seemed like I was the only one the dragon planned to save.

I pass Rain to Rune and kneel in front of the gentle monster's face, the hot breath coming from her nostrils making my eyes water.

We stare into each other's eyes for a minute in silence. I'm not sure what to say to my new yellow friend. Not how I knew to speak to the mother...

Wait.

I set my wand down in front of the dragon, her huge, glassy eyes following my motions as I do. The grass below my feet rustles as she takes sharp inhalations, sniffing at the dark stick I've laid before it.

I jump back a step when her forked tongue darts out, licking the wand once, then again, then wrapping around the wood casing. I worry for a second that I've just fed a dragon my most precious possession, but the tongue stays extended, snaking along the wand like a blind person studying brail. It's a strange, miraculous thing to watch.

I look back into the dragon's eyes and see tears starting to form.

She senses her mother.

"I promised your mother I'd save you," I say to the mythical beast, pretty confident my words won't fully register but sharing the sentiment all the same. "But now you've both saved me."

I look over at my partners in crime. Zev has a look of understanding, and I think Rune has pieced it together by now. AJ looks super baffled.

"I met this dragon's mom, right after Timót stole the baby away. She gave me the scale for my wand."

Things don't seem any clearer to AJ. "Did she like, sell it to you? Put it in an envelope and leave it at your door? Use eBay?"

"She *let* me take it," I say with a roll of my eyes. "She chose to let me go instead of burning me to death. That help?"

AJ shrugs, and it's as much of a yes as I can hope to get. I look back at the dragon and smile. "Thank you."

She releases my wand for me to retrieve, then I stand and join the others. "Let's get to some water and then go to... somewhere."

We take just a couple steps toward the edge of the grove before hearing the dragon rise to her feet, smashing a couple saplings with her tail as she does so. A few more steps and she starts to follow us.

Looks like we've got a new team member.

"Is this dragon like our pet now?" AJ asks. "God we're cool. Buncha magic bitches with a pet dragon."

Jokes aside, I do feel a little awesome. We escaped death, earned a dragon, and I've got my baby back. After I conjure a nifty harness for her out of thin air, I feel even better.

Naturally, that bit of happiness is fleeting. The sacrifice it took to get us free was perhaps the greatest I've ever witnessed. Erzsébet didn't have to die. She could have cast some spell, created some shadow, turned the air to ice--I don't know, done something to live and fight another day.

And while she gave her life willingly to help our cause, the wolves weren't so lucky. We brought terror to their once beautiful kingdom and it cost them everything.

I sense that Zev's thinking the same thing.

Not too far from the edge of the forest, we come to a small stream. AJ's already splashing in the shallow water before I know it's there. The dragon and Rune both kneel at the bank of the stream to drink, making quite the adorable pair. Like a boy as his dog.

I step over to Zev, who's staring at the water, lost in thought.

"Do you think any of them got away?"

He nods solemnly. "Wolves will fight until their last breath, but they won't die senselessly. I'm sure the ones that could, ran as the dragons came in."

That could be good news. "Where would they go?" I ask.

"I'm going to find out," he answers briskly as he leans down to take a drink of water.

I'm not sure what he means, and I'm mostly positive I won't like the answer.

"How do you plan on finding out?"

He steps up from the stream and gives me a deep, passionate kiss before pulling away and gazing at me with those enchanting green eyes.

"By finding them. I'll meet you in Aevelairith."

His words are still dancing along my eardrum and he's already shifted and started to sprint away as a wolf. He's lost in the trees before I can even think *get your self-sabotaging wolf ass back here!*

I know it's too late. He's gone and I could never convince him to stay anyway. I swallow my pride and sadness and get myself a drink from the stream. I have no idea how thirsty I am until the water hits my lips and I suck it down until my stomach feels full.

"So," I say as I fall back into the grass. "Back to the 'where the hell are we' question."

Rune plucks a few blades of grass, and I start to think he's going to throw them into the air like a golfer checking the wind, but then he does something even more strange and eats them.

"We gotta get Ru-Ru a sandwich, stat," AJ says, her short-term memory dismissing everything we've been through and getting right back to name calling. Fortunately Rune is too focused on his meal to hear the dig.

"Still to the south and east of Aevelairith, but only a short distance," he says with unflappable confidence. What the hell did he taste on that grass? "The stream will take us toward the main river."

In a different life, I'd yell for everyone to stop what they were doing so Rune could explain how a mouthful of plant and dirt worked as GPS, but now I just hop up, walk over to him for a quick, grassy-mouthed kiss, and start heading upstream.

No time like the present to stop trying to make sense of all this.

I only get a few steps forward before I stop, Darius' voice penetrating my mind.

I'm in the woods, safe from the sunlight. Turn to the left and you'll see me.

I spin almost too quickly, nearly tumbling backward into the stream. Through the trees, I can make out a figure.

"Wait here!" I yell to AJ and Rune as I sprint to my vampire. Rain was sleeping until this, but now her eyes are open as she tries to figure out why she's bouncing so much.

I reach Darius and take his face in my hands, kissing him all over his cheeks and lips.

"How did you get here?" I ask.

"Through the tunnels at first, then by staying beneath the canopy. I can travel when clouds pass or beneath the shade of a tree. It's not ideal, but it will do. More importantly, I've spoken with King Emerus, to tell him of these events."

I had forgotten about coordinating with the vampires. Now that the attacking has started, I wonder if it's already too late.

"He says the vampires will deploy immediately to aid our cause."

"That's great," I say, though I'm still wondering how it will all work out. "How are they getting here?"

Darius nods skeptically, picking up my tone. "They'll climb through the mountains as soon as the western sun sets. It's no short journey, but they'll move as fast as they can."

Okay cool. So we need to stay alive until at least nightfall. And we've got no time to lose. I kiss Darius again, then run back to my waiting travel companions.

They return to moving upstream as soon as I'm close, AJ riding on a wave she's created with her feet, looking like the happiest little girl in the world. The dragon, who I've started calling Sunflower, mostly walks alongside us and then occasionally bursts into the sky for a quick bit of flight.

Worry hits me every now and again that Timót and his army will descend on us without warning, but the calm of the others keeps me in check. Sunflower didn't take a straight route toward the fae kingdom, and I don't think my father will waste time searching every inch of the realm. Apparently he has eyes and ears all around, so he'll likely wait until he gets word.

Which is why the sooner we get to Aevelairith, the sooner we need to prepare for war.

My fear leads me down a path of reflection, as memories of the earliest days with the Sexies pop into my mind. I'd never known terror like I felt being trapped in my bar with those three strangers, and now I'll never know a life without them. We're either together, or I die.

I think about arriving in Budapest and meeting

the queen of the witches, how her riddles frustrated and flustered me, but her patience and care made me into a powerful witch. Within my magic, I'll always carry a part of Erzsébet. And so will Rain.

I think about my parents, both deadset on ruining my life for different bad reasons. Mom because magic had cost her so much, and dad because he's always felt slighted by those better than him. What a terrible pair of parents. Maybe if they'd stayed together they'd have balanced each other out. Or killed each other earlier and saved me all this trouble.

In the distance, I see the mountainous walls that surround the valleys of Aevelairith. If there was a kingdom I had to fight in, and perhaps die in, this would be it. I feel the power of the earth moving below my feet. The old magic of the Fates is sowed into the soil here. In the strangest way, this land feels like home.

Our small stream merges with the river and we begin the final leg of what might be our final journey. I don't expect to go on another quest before we have to put our lives on the line to save the Last Witch, my pure and innocent baby, from those who would treat her as a magical prize to be coveted and captured.

When we reach the gate leading into the kingdom, no guard stands watch. It's eerie after our first visit, even if we did arrive as naked prisoners.

Rune quickly scales the wall and sets the gears in motion to open the stone barrier.

Inside, it's like a ghost town. A night ago there was merriment at every stop, and now it's like the people have gone into hiding. They probably have, but I'm not sure what Revia told them to hide from.

"I assume the fae are gathered at the Cliff of Liliolyn," Rune says. "To send my parents' ashes off to be with their ancestors."

He starts marching through the kingdom with a purposeful stride. Sunflower takes to the sky overhead while AJ and I follow our leader.

We walk to the outer edge of the city and then turn off on a path leading up a golden hillside. As we walk, the distant sound of humming and chanting can be heard. It gets louder as we approach the top of the hill, and then all of the fae are suddenly before us.

They stand overlooking a cliff, with two caskets resting at the edge of the precipice. It's a solemn, focused ceremony, so they don't notice our approach.

They do, however, hear the sound of beating dragon wings as Sunflower crests the hilltop.

There are cries and screams at first, but the crowd

settles when they see Rune, standing with his hand raised. I have no idea if anyone here still trusts him, but the fact that he's calmly standing in front of a dragon means people will at least hear him out.

"Revia is dead," Rune announces.

"You killed her too!" a voice shouts from the crowd.

"I killed no one," the fae prince answers calmly. "Your king and queen were killed by the same blindness that's been murdering the fae for generations. The mindless adherence to a prophecy that no longer holds true. My mother and father finally saw the error of our ways, and for that, Revia killed them."

Lots of murmurs. Lots of head shaking. It wouldn't surprise me if this turned into an angry mob situation, so I keep my wand at the ready.

"We have a new enemy now," Rune says. "He and his army ride on the back of dragons. He'll be in Aevelairith by nightfall, perhaps sooner. We have no choice but to defend our kingdom until our blood runs dry."

"Our greatest fighters have fled," a woman yells out. "Gone in search of you."

Rune nods. "I know. They were tricked and killed by the man of which I speak. That's why…"

I'm pretty sure Rune was going to mention the

fact that a bunch of vampires might show up, but the arrival of Zev in wolf form cuts him off. He shifts to human as people scream and gasp but make no move to attack. Perhaps his nudity and impressive manhood keeps everyone distracted.

Alden died in the attack, Zev whispers to me. *Mother perished as well. The remaining wolves will regroup and come to fight alongside their new king.*

I take Zev's hand and squeeze it tightly. The loss might sting, but right now he's focused on a greater good. I love him for that, even as my heart breaks for him. He's lost his whole family in under a day, and now must go to war. That shit is not easy to process.

The werewolf stands between me and Rune, also taking the fae's hand in a show of solidarity. Rune smiles and then returns to addressing the crowd.

"We may be joined by vampires tonight," he says to more gasps from the crowd. He looks at Zev, who nods. "And wolves. Those we fought for so long, Fates willing, shall come and take up arms beside us. To protect Aevelairith. And to protect the Last Witch."

The people are silent, with the soundtrack for this heavy moment just the steady beating of Sunflower's wings. They see Rain strapped to me, the prophetic baby alive and well. I try to smile at anyone willing to make eye contact. To show we're not the enemy.

Finally, a tall, elderly fae steps forward.

"What would you have us do, my liege?"

Rune smiles, relieved that he won't have to do anymore arguing or convincing. For now.

"First, we send my parents to join the ancestors. We mourn our loss and give them our blessings."

The fae nod, support for their new leader growing.

"And then," Rune continues, "we prepare to fight as though our entire world depends on it, for it truly does."

CHAPTER SEVENTEEN

I pace the war room--which is really just a cool way of describing the room with all the maps and little toy soldiers--as I think through a convoluted and twisty plan that has more holes in it than swiss cheese--or my brain after childbirth.

Darius arrived shortly after the fae said a final goodbye to Rivelis and Scocha. I found him lurking in the shadows just at the bottom of the hill. With our group at full strength, Rune led us into this small but impressive space, within the trunk of a mighty oak tree.

I keep pouring over the maps laid out on the large stone table the five of us are sitting around. Well six, if you count my baby. There are little fae, wolf and vampire wooden figurines spread over the different kingdoms. I wonder who carved these? We don't have any dragons, so AJ helpfully made a few tiny paper airplanes to represent them. Though she keeps stealing them from the table to launch at Zev's stoic face.

He ignores her, but when his thoughts bleed into mine I have to hold back an inappropriate laugh.

I offered to find a piece of shit to stand in for daddy dearest, but that idea got rejected.

Vaemore, the vampire kingdom, is located in the Northeast region of the world. The fae kingdom of Aevelairith sits opposite them in the Northwest region, and Wiceraweil is directly below the fae in the Southwest region. There's a massive mountain range running down the center, cutting the vampires off from the rest. It's part of what allows them to bespell their territory in magical sunblock.

I keep looking at the map, trying to think of a place we might run to, a way we can escape and join forces with the other races, then get the high ground. No matter how I slice it, no such place exists. For one, it's kind of hard to get a higher ground than dragons.

Timót will come through the air, with an army that dwarfs ours. Fighting in Aevelairith is our best bet. And the odds really aren't that good.

"I'm working on an idea," I tell the guys. "But I don't think you'll like it."

They already have their eyes narrowed, trying to read my thoughts and feelings, ready to dissuade me of any suggestions that sound risky. Unfortunately for them, the window for avoiding risk got shattered back in Rowley.

"We need a plan that's better than 'fight and win'," I say. "We don't know when or how many of the wolves and vampires will show up. We're assuming my father will arrive soon, but 'soon' is our best guess. We have one dragon. He's got dozens. We've got a decimated fae army that doesn't know who to trust. Our plan can't rely on brute strength. We have to be smarter than that." I look down at Rain, blissfully unaware of this chaotic world that's so obsessively aware of her. "We need to lure him in."

The guys look disgusted. I turn to AJ for backup, but she's frowning. "I don't like it," she says, but before I can chew her out for not taking my side, she holds up a hand and takes Rain from me, giving the baby's head kisses. "But I think you're right. We have to try."

The Sexies are none too happy, but appeasing them really isn't the goal.

I take Rain back and hold her close to my chest,

marveling at what a calm, sweet little thing she is despite everything.

I mean, I'd take a bout of colic or cradle cap over someone constantly trying to kill my poor kid, but I'm insanely grateful she is such a perfect little peanut.

I kiss her nose, then get back to it. "We don't know how long we have. Rune, I assume the fae have a system of defense in place given all your warring?"

He nods. "We do, but not against dragons. Fighting off an aerial attack will be a very different thing than targeting vampires or wolves."

"You have archers?" Zev asks.

"Yes. The best left with Revia, but we still have some."

"Let's use em," I say, studying a different map that shows the outer walls of the fae kingdom. "We don't know which direction he'll come from, do we? If they flew straight from Wiceraweil, they'd already be here."

"We don't, but we can control the ease with which they fly into our kingdom," Rune says.

I smile, sensing the direction he's going. "So we can make giant illusions?"

Rune nods. "With enough fae working in concert, we can make the kingdom disappear... for a brief while."

"Then how will the vamps and wolves find us?" AJ asks, pointing out the big flaw in my plan.

"That's a problem," I admit, looking around the table, hoping someone smarter than me has an idea I haven't thought of.

When no one immediately speaks up, I give it my best shot. "Can the illusion just work from the bird's eye view? So anything approaching on foot doesn't have to deal with it?""

Rune scratches his chin. "Yes, as long as everyone casting the charm takes the same approach. Though it won't be as strong of an illusion."

I shrug. "I think we have to risk it. We need all the help we can get."

Rune nods. "We shall make it so."

I look back at the map but I'm not really seeing it. My mind is on the inevitable showdown between me and my father, and no drawing or figurines will help with that. The others sense where my head is at, but none of them has an easy solution.

"I need to lead my father into the tunnels below the city," I say, voicing this realization before I've had much time to process it. "Fending off the dragons is important, but we need to get to Timót. Cut off the head, kill the beast."

"And if his dragons cave in the tunnels, crushing

you and your child?" Darius asks, his dark eyes piercing me.

"Timót's only here for Rain," I say. "Yeah, he wants to kill everyone who might stand in his way, but none of it matters to him without the Last Witch. He won't let his own army hurt the baby."

"Then we'll come with you to the tunnels," Zev says, determined to shield me from harm as much as possible.

I shake my head. "He's an immortal with a dragon armor suit and a lifetime of witch training. If there's an obstacle he doesn't mind killing, he'll kill it. Besides, you three will have your hands full. You have to defeat his army... with or without help."

"And how do you expect to destroy a being too powerful for any of us?" Darius asks in his righteous way.

I shrug. It's not like I fancy myself an equal match against my father, or consider myself stronger than anyone in this room. Experience-wise, I'm the least equipped for this fight. The one advantage I have is that he'll hesitate before killing me, and take every step not to hurt my baby. I think back on my lessons with Erzsébet, and while nothing sticks out as the perfect solution, I trust the magic will find me.

"Annnnnnnd, does anyone have any use for the

water nymph?" AJ jokes, but she probably is feeling a little left out. She likes to drive the action, though she recognizes we're not fighting in her best arena.

"I need you to just stay alive," I say. "If something happens to me, but we somehow save Rain, I need you here for her." The pressure of the moment keeps me from crying, but it doesn't stop AJ. She hides her face and gives me a thumbs up.

We sit in silence, processing the strategy I've just thrown together on the fly. I'm not sure when I took charge of the mission, and I'm alarmed that my scheme has me facing our most powerful rival all on my own. That's the way it has to be, though. And that's why it fell on me to propose the master plan. No one else is willing to put me in harm's way.

"So... what does everyone think?" I don't really want feedback but I need to break the silence.

"How will you draw Timót into the tunnels?" Rune asks. "He'll see the same illusion as the rest, provided it works."

I've got a half-baked thought for this, and I'm hoping everyone can help me cook it all the way through. "Can we, if I'm able to do the crazy thing I'm thinking of doing, create the illusion right after my father and I land on the ground? Before the rest of the dragons arrive?"

"Theoretically," Rune says in a voice that still needs some convincing.

"Let's say, hypothetically, I take to the sky on our dragon. We know she's fast enough to outrun the pack, and we know Timót won't send one of his goons after me instead of giving chase himself. As soon as he and I cross a certain threshold, can the fae throw up the illusion and confuse the shit out of everyone else?"

Zev and Darius both turn to Rune, clearly employing a pressure campaign to make him say it's impossible. The more I talk about using myself as bait, the angrier the thoughts of my lovers become.

Rune's too devoted to logic to cave. "Yes, we can. We'll confuse the shit right out of them."

Nothing diffuses the tension like Rune doing a little human talk.

Both Darius and Zev try to plead with my mind, begging for another solution, but I reject every effort. My gut hasn't led me astray yet, and I don't see another path forward.

"No more time to waste," I say. "I love you all very, very much."

It might undercut the power of my previous speech, but I need to get gushy for just a quick second. I'm scared to death of what's about to happen, so I'm taking this chance to tell them how I feel. In case another chance doesn't come around.

Darius kisses me deeply before disappearing into the shadows.

Zev takes his turn next, nuzzling my neck after his kiss, nipping at the bite mark he used to claim me.

And then Rune takes me into his arms. His eyes are a mix of sadness and strength. So much has happened to him in the last day, it seems unfair that he could still endure more pain. I make a silent promise that he won't experience another loss.

God I hope I can keep my word.

Rune kisses me tenderly, holding my face as he does, and then he brushes away a tear I didn't know I had before running off to prepare the fae.

I sniff, then take AJs hand and lead us to the garden Rune shared with me just a couple nights before. There are small streams and so much beautiful plant life, it seems like this is where AJ should be. Sunflower sits just outside the garden walls, looking like an adorable, enormous, scaled puppy.

AJ and I stroll over to the Tree of Life, neither of us able to speak. This is the hardest goodbye to say because AJ doesn't have a task to busy herself with. She just gets to watch me walk away and then hope for the best.

I hug my best friend and kiss her cheek. "Stay safe. Don't do anything stupid."

Now we're both crying, but the bitch uses her magic to make her tears change shapes and dance around, to a delighted cry from Rain. "You've impressed your god daughter," I say with a wet laugh.

There are more hugs and tears and kisses. And then it's time.

"I'm proud of you, B," she says, just as I turn to leave. "A real queen."

I pause and smile at her through wet lashes. But I don't turn around to look at her again.

I can't.

Destiny is calling.

And for that, I need a dragon.

Sunflower is waiting for me when I step out of the garden. When she sees me and Rain, she stands, unfurls her wings and lowers her head so that I can mount her more easily.

And then we are off. I've got the baby tightly strapped to my chest, knowing we might be in for a bumpy ride. As we soar into the clouds, my heart lurches and my pulse speeds up from sheer nerves. I really hope this plan works.

I direct the dragon in a sweeping circle around the kingdom, so we can cautiously scout to see what direction my father's army will be coming from. It shouldn't be hard to spot an entire thunder of dragons coming at us; the hard part will be making sure they don't spot us first.

The wind rushes through my hair, and with nothing but clouds around me I feel at once free and terrified. The moments of solitude help me settle my mind, and I pat the dragon as we soar through the sky. "I lost my mom too," I tell her, though my voice hardly carries with the wind. "Maybe we can be each other's family now," I say, though lord help me I have no idea what I'd do with a dragon at Morgan's Pub.

It makes me wonder: what *is* going to happen to us all once this is over, should we survive to the end? It's a question that plagues me, even though there's so much danger that stands between myself and an answer. I wish I could spare a few moments to think about the long term, or to spend time with Darius alone to help him process his torment. Or with Zev and Rune who should be busy grieving right now.

It's all been put on hold for a senseless war, and I hate it. I want this over with. I want it done. I want my father out of my life forever. Out of all of our lives. It would be real nice if this were a normal dad problem that could be solved with a block button rather than a whole war.

Then my thoughts wander back to the task at hand, and the possible outcomes of today. Each more gruesome than the last.

As my thoughts turn dangerously dark, the dragon beneath me stops short, nearly toppling me from her back.

I see in the distance the glint of dragon scale against the fading sun just as my dragon whips around and begins flying slowly towards the underground entry to the tunnels.

I wait, twisted in the seat with my wand at the ready.

I don't take action until I can see my father's eyes.

Until I know he can see his coveted prize.

I kiss my sweet girl on the head, trying to show that I love her despite what's about to happen.

And then I blast a firebolt at him from my wand, and we race off through the sky, the wind piercing as my father gives chase.

The other dragons follow, but my father stays well in the lead. So far, so good, even though it all feels mostly bad.

"Hurry," I whisper to the dragon as I lean forward, trying to make my body more aerodynamic. Being a lumpy human meat suit holding a baby does little to decrease air resistance.

We are nearing the planned disembarkment site, and my nerves are frayed. I clutch the bundle to my chest with one hand, and raise my wand with the other as my dragon lands and I slide off in a fluid motion that's movie quality, if I do say so myself.

I make the mistake of looking behind me to see if my father has caught up. The lightning bolt that explodes the ground at my feet indicates he has indeed.

Bastard.

I climb down through the tunnel door and speed along the dark passage, knowing my dad will follow. I try to keep my strides smooth, not wanting to bounce Rain too much and make her scream.

The deeper in we go, the narrower the tunnel, which works to our advantage. I stop when I reach a cavern with a few different exits. I plan on walking out of here the victor, but I'd at least like to keep the option to run away available.

I face the opening nervously, my wand drawn, my back straight. I try not to shake.

My father arrives on foot and alone, just as I'd hoped. He stands taller than life with his dragon skin armor. Just seeing him in such an atrocity makes my stomach lurch.

The earth around us shakes as he approaches, and

he looks up and smiles. "It sounds like my dragons have started the attack. You have the power to end this and save many lives."

I want to brag, to showboat all the ways we are keeping his dragons confused, but that would be stupid and ego-driven. I keep my face stoic and say a silent prayer everything is going okay up there. I have to trust the Sexies to handle the battle above while I fight my own down here.

"Give me the child," he says, holding out his hands like I'm just going to do what he says, no biggie. "I won't harm her. She will grow up to be the witch queen, ruling every realm, with me the Grand Emperor of all."

"Forgive me if your penchant for murder doesn't instill the utmost trust for my daughter's safety." And then, because I don't want to make the mistake of every villain in every B movie and spend too much time talking, I unleash my wand into my father, fully determined to strike first.

He draws just as quickly, a counterspell causing my fire to fizzle without doing any harm.

"You mistake raw magic and luck for power, Bernadette," he says, slowly stepping closer. "I'm sure the witch queen tried to get you to understand your magic, but she didn't teach you the control it takes to be powerful."

A spark flies from the tip of his wand and slices my shoulder before I can react. The pain is hard to bear, but I'm even more concerned that a strap on the harness has been cut. Once he gets Rain away from me, I've lost my child... and my leverage.

"I know these things because I was in your shoes, hoping to learn how to harness these powers, yet being taught nothing. Erzsébet spent centuries blaming the other races for the downfall of the witches, when it was their own hubris and pretension that led us to where we are now."

Another spark flies from his wand, but this time I'm ready to deflect. A bubble of light forms around my wand and saves my right arm from the same injury as my left. However, in the moments I waste celebrating my success, Timót fires another shot that tears into my hip, breaking another strap and cutting deep into my flesh. I drop to a knee, fighting through the searing pain so I can keep an eye on my father as he steps even closer.

When another tremor pulls my father's attention to the cavern walls above us, I try to sneak in another shot. As soon as I mutter *tűz*, he moves his wand in a small circle and sends the fire back toward me. I fall to the ground, covering Rain to keep her from burning while I feel the heat run across my back.

I'm outmatched. Timót's envisioned this fight for decades, and my list of spells is maybe three pages long. My heart was in the right place bringing this final battle to my doorstep, but I'm out of my depth.

I hear his footsteps getting closer. I don't fear for my life, not yet. I only fear for my baby. For the life he'll force her to live. I've brought her to this moment, hoping things would go my way in the end. I wanted so badly to offer the protection no one offered me. I think back to my mother, devastated by her powers, betrayed by her magic, trying to take her own life to save the others around her. I fight back tears, hating even the inkling of sympathy I might feel for that woman.

My father stands right behind me, leaning down to put a hand on my shoulder.

"Despite what you may think, I don't want to hurt you. I want you to raise your child in the *Érintett* Kingdom, to discover at last the powers you possess, and to pass those gifts on to your daughter. I fight to give you what's best, Bernadette."

I slowly rise from the ground, first to my knees, keeping an arm wrapped around Rain so she won't fall from her carrier. I slowly get to my feet and turn to face Timót, not making any move to back away from him.

"I guess that's the difference between us," I say as I raise my wand, just inches from his face.

He keeps his eyes locked on mine and brings his wand up to eye level, the two tips glowing as the competing powers push and pull against each other.

"What's that?" he asks, the light from our wands flickering in his eyes hiding behind the dragonskin mask.

"You'll kill everyone to try and keep us alive. I'll kill us to make sure you can't hurt anyone else."

My wand has been aimed at his eyes, and he's ready to defend himself. What he's not prepared for is me turning the wand toward my chest.

Toward me.

Toward Rain.

His eyes go wide, confused and afraid of whatever I might do. He doesn't even react as I grab him by the shoulder and pull him into a tight embrace, summoning all the strength of a mother who's had enough.

"Goodbye," I whisper into my dad's ear. Then I scream "*dominálnak lélek!*"

And the world goes white.

CHAPTER EIGHTEEN

I t's quiet.

I don't hear, see, smell or feel anything.

My mind is like a blank slate, the only thought running through is the awareness that I have no thoughts.

The space around me is incredibly bright, but it doesn't hurt my eyes or force me to squint. Ever so slowly, the white glare begins to fade, replaced by a soft yellow. Walls start to come into view as a room takes shape around me. I notice that I'm in a chair, comfortably seated, my wand in my hand.

My baby strapped to my chest.

"We don't control our magic."

Erzsébet sits in front of me, just a few feet away

and not at all dead. She carries on with a casual lesson, her voice calm and soothing.

"Instead, we become it. This is why powers take time, and spells don't get thought up overnight." She stops talking for a moment to look at Rain and make a silly face, eliciting a cute little giggle.

"When you first arrived in Budapest, it wasn't simply that you couldn't control your powers, Bernie. That's too simple a solution. That's what some... less thoughtful witches--and others--might have you believe."

I know she's talking about my father. But I also know this conversation is taking place during our trainings, back before I took the portal to Vaemor, before I knew anything of my father's plans.

"You have to think of controlling magic the same way you think of taking a breath. Or looking into the sky. Or enjoying a friendship. You simply do those things, because your body and your heart and your mind are part of your greater being. So too is your magic."

More thoughts crystalize in my mind as she speaks. I've just traveled through all of the kingdoms, running and fighting and hurting and loving. I've just been in the darkness, hugging my baby tight, trying to protect her.

To save her from Timót.

"The more you let magic bind with you, the more it becomes who you are and what you can do. The more you become it. The longer you grow with your powers, the greater your abilities. Eventually, the spells and knowledge live in your body as part of your genetic makeup, more than just an education. The power comes to your aid when you need it, not simply because you can recite an incantation. Your wand, special and useful as it may be, becomes less important."

I'm in the tomb in Budapest. This is a lesson from Erzsébet.

But I'm in the tunnel with Timót, our bodies closed around Rain as magic explodes around us.

That's where I really am. My mind, however, is walking through a memory.

"If I teach you nothing else, dear girl, let this lesson get through to you," the queen says, leaning in close. "Magic binds to nothing so tightly as love. It is more than a feeling. It is at the core of who you are, and it is a very tangible thing in the magical world. Love has kept you alive, has brought three very powerful men to your side. In your time of greatest need, it is where you will find your greatest power."

The white light slowly returns, and the smiling

witch before me is washed away by the brightness. The senses I once lacked start to return, bit by bit. Smells, tastes, sounds. Pain. Tremendous, glorious pain. Tremendous because it's so strong I want to pass out; glorious because, looking into the lifeless eyes of Timót, his head on the cavern floor next to mine, I know he can't feel it.

As I slowly regain consciousness, I'm riding a wave of numbness and traveling at superspeed. Darius has me in his arms, sprinting me through the tunnel.

I lean my head against his chest. I can't use my arms or hands. Everything hurts as the adrenaline fades and the pain hits hard and fast.

I moan in his arms and he holds me closer, his voice a calm presence in my mind. *You'll be okay. It's all okay. You're going to be fine.*

I don't know if I believe him. I hardly trust I'm alive right now, much less that I will continue living for the next few minutes.

As we run, Darius makes me drink some of his blood. It drips into my mouth and then runs down my cheek. I don't have the power to swallow.

His cheeks are stained with tears as he carries me out of the tunnels and to the secret garden. I can hardly see, but the smell of the plants and the feel of cool night air comes as a welcome relief.

The sound of battle is loud around us. I don't know if Darius has been weaving between warring factions or if the fight is further away. I've lost the ability to focus on anything, and I trust him to avoid the worst of it.

In the distance, I hear a howl. Zev, perhaps? Then I hear another, and another, and more howling voices until it sounds like a whole pack.

"Wolves?" I say, my voice barely above a whisper.

Darius reaches an empty patch of grass and sets me down gently. He sees my flesh wounds, but I think he knows that's not where the real damage is.

"Yes," he answers. "They arrived just before the flash of lightning shot up from the ground. I came to you as fast as I could."

I try to ask Darius what's happening, but he just shushes me and tells me it'll all be fine.

Except I can tell he's lying.

He knows I'm dying.

And so do I. I summoned a spell to challenge every soul in that family embrace. I unleashed powers great enough to bring down the living dead.

I thought that maybe magic bound by love could somehow live on.

Hopefully in Rain. I'm not sure I'll be around long enough to find out.

My head rolls to the side and I see the Tree of Life, standing tall above me. I wish I could have lain beneath it in earlier times, before the witches died, when magic flowed freely.

I hear footsteps as AJ cries out and runs over to kneel beside us. She reaches down and starts to carefully unstrap Rain.

"What happened? What do you need me to do, B?" She asks through her tears.

"Is she alive?" I ask with what little breath I have left as my friend cradles my baby. Even as I ask, I'm afraid I don't want the answer.

AJ stifles a sob as she lifts Rain. "I... don't know."

"Can you lay her on my chest?" I ask. "Put her little head under my chin." As AJ sets my baby down, I flash back to her birth, the first time I held her in my arms.

For every first, there is a last. And I have reached mine.

"What happened," AJ whispers. Thankfully, Darius answers on my behalf.

"The ground beneath our feet lit up, then I raced into the tunnels. I found Bernie and Rain beside Timót. Both their wands were shattered."

I hear a howl coming closer to us, and then Zev is here, shifting from wolf to man. "Bernie," he falls to his knees at my side, his expression matching Darius.

Rune arrives seconds later, probably having guessed I caused the flash. He looks angry and sad and all the things I can't deal with because my life is fading really fast and I'm about to feel the touch of my daughter for the last time and I can't bear it.

Tears slide down my face as my arms lay uselessly at my side, my fingers dusted with dirt.

"You all need to help the wolves" I manage to croak. No sense in watching me die while Aevelairith burns.

"The vampires arrived," Zev says. "Seconds after the sun settled behind the hills."

Thank God. Emerus held true to his word. That gives me a bit of hope not just for this fight, but for the future of the kingdoms when this battle is done.

He did keep his word, Darius says, picking up on my thoughts. *He was the first over the mountains, leading his men like a true king.*

I wish I could thank him, I say back.

You cannot, Darius says sternly. *He died in the dragons' fire. And you will not go to the other side to meet him.*

Poor Darius. So many years of immortality, and

now so much death. Cara, father, brother... and now, me.

Rune looks to the sky and I follow his gaze. In the air I see dozens of massive dragons. It's a sight that would bring terror, except they're flying in the opposite direction.

"The dragons are leaving," the fae says. "It appears they've left without the *Érintett*."

"Timót's wand," Darius says softly. "You broke the spell and set them free."

That brings a blip of happiness into my heart. Those beautiful beasts deserve much better. I also find some peace in knowing my beloveds might not die today. But the feeling is fleeting as I look back at the Tree of Life, in dire need of magic only my kind can provide. While the different interpretations of the prophecy might have been off base, the truth remains that this world's magic is in short supply.

I have no wand. I have no strength. I need a miracle.

You are the miracle, a voice in my mind whispers. A voice who is decidedly not either of my mates.

Who are you? I ask, wondering if this is the voice of death come to take me to meet AJ's beau.

You know who I am, she says. *Look upon me.*

My eyes are on the trunk of the massive tree, but I

let them drift up toward the foliage. While nothing stands out as drastically different, I notice for the first time a face, made of branches and leaves. It might have always been there, but I can only see it now because it's talking to me.

Am I dead?

You could be, she says. *Do you want to be?*

No.

Then live on.

The skin above my heart burns anew, even though I thought my body was done feeling pain. This is a different sort of agony, though. And it strikes me at a particular point--right where the Dryad queen punctured me. My heart rate increases, and I feel blood trickling from my wounds and dropping onto the earth below me.

Ah yes, I know your blood, the tree says. *It is of the Fate who planted me, and who breathed life into the fae.*

My blood?

The leaves of the tree shake, like it's nodding. *You have the blood of a creator. One of the givers of life.*

My family's blood? My family traces back to one of the Fates?

That's right, sweet girl.

This is a new voice, and it's one I recognize in an instant.

Tilly…

There's a new face in the tree, one that somehow, while still made of twigs and leaves, looks just like my beautiful nanny.

Our magic flourished in this garden and in these woods, nanny says. *I think the Tree of Life is happy to see you here.*

It's then I notice that the talking tree, with faces made of branches, has started to regain its glow. My eyes drift back down, and I see my magic surging through my hands and into the ground.

You found the love we'd all been searching for, Bernie, Tilly says. *It's bound to you, and your magic to it.*

I didn't want to hurt Rain, I say in my mind while tears stream down my face. *I didn't want either of us to die, Nanny. I'm not like my mother.*

Of course you're not. That's exactly why you're going to be alright.

Even in the tree, Tilly has the sweetest smile.

You won't be seeing me anytime soon. Wake up, she says.

Wake up, the Tree of Life repeats.

Wake up.

Bernie, wake up. Bernie!

Love!

The voices no longer belong to the faces in the tree, but rather to Darius and Zev. I can feel arms clutching me as I jolt up. I've got my arms wrapped around Rain, and as I feel my breath come back, I can hear my baby's heartbeat. She's alive.

I look at Rune, whose face is drenched with tears, his eyes locked on the Tree of Life.

The beautiful, vibrant, *living* Tree of Life.

White and golden light runs through the trunk, spilling out of the branches, bringing the tree back to life. I look down at my hands, at my body, and see the magic still pulses through me and into the soil beneath my fingertips.

Glancing back at the tree, I can just barely make out the outline of the face. A gust of wind rustles the leaves, but I know it's a smile.

Rune looks in awe as he speaks. "You brought her back to life, Bernie."

Without looking away from the tree, I reach out and take Rune's hand, swapping some of my Fate-forged magic for his eternal calm. "*We* brought her back to life," I say as I look at Rain, her sweet face lighting up my heart brighter than any sparkling tree.

Darius stands, looking off into the distance.

"I hear cheers," Zev says, filling the rest of us in on the sounds only a wolf can hear.

"Yes," Darius says. "I can sense it in the vampire soldiers. The *Érintett* have surrendered."

I squeeze and kiss my child, then take a moment to look at each of my Sexy companions and my dearest friend.

The war is over.

We get to start the rest of our lives.

"So, a werewolf, a vampire and a fae walk into a bar..." Frank says, as he sloshes his Guinness before taking another sip. Frank's a beefy type, with a thick body and a thick dark beard that covers his aging skin. He was a truck driver for 40 years and is now a professional barfly at my pub.

"Does that joke even have an ending?" Phil asks from a barstool a few seats down. Between them is a pint of beer. Every night they buy one in memory of Joe--who died in a way they'll never know the full truth of--and leave it in his regular spot, regardless of how busy Morgan's gets.

Frank shrugs. "That's what I'm trying to find out. I figure if I start the joke enough times, someone will finish it and then we'll finally know how it ends."

I feel the sting of a hand towel slapping my ass and turn to glare at AJ. "Bitch!"

She just sticks out her tongue, then looks to Frank.

"A werewolf, a vampire, and a fae walk into a bar..." she says. "And then everyone falls in love."

Frank frowns and then takes a long pull of his beer. "I don't get it."

I laugh. "It's got a lot of layers, Frank. Give it some time."

"Hey Bernie, when you gonna play for us again?" Phil asks as he raises his glass to his lips.

"Soon!" I glance at my beautiful piano and sigh. There hasn't been enough time for my music, though I have been working on a related project whenever I get a spare moment.

The bell above our door dings and Alice, Frank's wife, comes in, sees her husband, and beelines to the bar, avoiding Joe's seat to take the stool on the other side of Frank. "Bernie, where's that beautiful baby of yours? I have a gift for her."

Alice pulls a lovely knitted blanket from her purse and hands it to me. It's pink with tiny blue unicorns designed into it.

I hold it to my chest and smile. "Thank you, this

is beautiful. She's with her dads right now, but I'll have her here with me tomorrow."

AJ snorts. "*Dads*. Spoiled little witch," she says under her breath.

Alice raises an eyebrow, and leans in like we're going to have a private conversation--but everyone can still hear us. "Are you really going to keep seeing all three of those men? And let all of them raise your child?"

This has been an ongoing conversation for the last five months, because of course it is. This is Rowley and I walk around with three dudes on my arm. Whatever. Let the people talk.

"Yes, I'm really dating them all, and yes, they are all taking the role as father for Rain." They've certainly earned it.

Alice gives me a skeptical, judgy look, but then follows it up with the perfect question. "Does that mean the dark-haired one won't be dancing for us anymore?" she asks.

AJ howls with laughter and I really wish Darius was here to answer for himself. "Oh, he'll still dance. I'm not the jealous type. I'm happy to share my eye candy with the world."

I squint at the time and sigh. "Okay, last call folks. I've got a meeting to get to."

Frank looks like I've just informed him he has a terminal illness. "But Bernie, it's too early to call it a night. Christ, it's still light out!" He legit looks like he might cry.

Alice nudges her husband. "How about we take the party home? We've got beer in the fridge and we can rewatch one of the Pats' Super Bowl wins."

The idea of beer and football on his own couch cheers Frank up, so much so that he leaves half a pint unfinished as he chases his wife out the bar, both of them giggling like school children. God bless small town New England folk.

Phil, the last one left, leaves cash on the bar and nods his head. "See you tomorrow. Good luck with that... meeting." He eyes me like he knows more than he's letting on, but I know for a fact he's clueless.

Hell, even I'm living in suspended disbelief. I wake up every morning wondering if this is actually my life.

Once I've locked the front door and turned the sign to closed, I meet AJ at the door leading down to the basement. We're totally in a hurry, but I still hesitate. I need a moment to look around Morgan's, to soak up some nostalgia before I take this next step.

"Don't stress," AJ says. "You're not saying goodbye, you're just... leaving for a minute."

"Sure," I say with a little eye roll. "Let's go with that. Got my makeup?"

AJ nods and then follows me downstairs to the basement. At first glance, this place looks like it always has. Dusty and stacked with extra supplies for the bar. The only notable difference is a big book shelf with a locked glass door. It's full of books of spells that I wanted to keep close at hand as I continue my magical studies.

The most important difference, however, hides within the inner-workings of my old piano. It's been down here since the Sexies went all Extreme Home Makeover back when they first arrived. Over the last few months, I've been engaged in some heavy magical lifting. First I had to enchant each key on the keyboard. Then I had to create spells that were summoned with musical chords instead of recited words. Lastly, I had to bend space and time to cater to the songs played on my childhood piano. Here in my basement, under my family bar that secretly housed generations of witches, I've created a portal to multiple realms.

It's been the craziest undertaking of my magical career, and apparently the entire magical world is floored by my efforts. Perhaps the wildest part is that I did it all without my wand. I've found that since I died and came back, my power lives within me and doesn't need a conduit to do my bidding. My magic is always available to me, and more and more I'm learning control of it.

AJ sits on the bench next to me and I start to play. It's a newer piece, written with elements of Hungarian music and then little influences from each of the kingdoms of the other world. As I play, the bench below us starts to glow, and a ring of light forms a circle around me and AJ.

When I whisper the word *"Sulvara,"* we're whisked away to another world.

We step out of the blinding light inside a cluster of trees behind the back entrance to a sprawling, stone estate. This portal leads straight to the heart of Sulvara Castle, the newly established kingdom of the witches… and all other magical creatures. The name itself was pulled from the Hungarian words for magic and unity.

This portal was the easiest and first I created. The hardest part has been negotiating with the werewolves, vampires and fae regarding portal use and placement. Magic returning to the realm has helped a lot with easing tensions, but it'll take more than a few months and a commitment to peace for trust to be rebuilt.

That's what I'm working hard on, and today will bring us a step closer.

I hope.

Before my eyes even clear from the blinding light, my best friend is dragging me toward an open door with witches standing guard at either side.

"No time to lose, B. Do you know how much work you need to look good tonight?" she asks.

"Gee thanks, A."

She nudges me through the door, and we both smile politely as the witches gesture for us to go in. We keep moving at a good clip until we reach the kitchen. It's packed with castle staff who are putting the final touches together for the feast planned after the ceremony.

I smile at the head chef, a young witch with a knack for the culinary. "Tressa, everything looks and smells outrageous. Can I sample anything"

She beams at the praise and reaches for a small puff pastry, but AJ pushes me forward before I can take it.

"Not now, we need to move."

Sad and hungry, I let my dearest, meanest friend direct me up a spiral staircase and then down another long hall. At the end of it is a double-door leading into my suite.

My eyes light up as I open the door and see Rain sitting on the ground--all by herself!--playing with a dragon plushie someone at the pub gave her.

She looks every bit a princess dressed in sheer peach tulle with tiny embroidered flowers. I coo at her and crawl to face her. "How's the best little girl in all the worlds?" I ask as she reaches her chubby hands to cup my cheeks and giggles.

I kiss her and sit up, smiling at Rune, Darius and Zev--the dad sitters today. "How was daddy day care?" I ask, noting that my powerful men all look a little tired, but still entirely enamored with baby Rain.

"She's a genius," Rune declares proudly.

"She's strong," Zev says combatively.

"She's clever," Darius says with a wink, and I can't help but laugh at the three of them.

"She's a little of each of you," I reassure them. "Now, you all need to kiss me and scat so I can get dressed." I look down at my jeans and T-shirt ensemble. "I don't think this is gonna cut it."

They stand to go, with Rune leaning in to take Rain, but I stop him. "Let her stay. I miss her, and besides, she might as well learn early the great pains women take to look beautiful. Maybe she'll be the generation that puts an end to this nonsense."

AJ rolls her eyes. "There is nothing nonsense about wanting to present the most beautiful artistry in your appearance."

"Agree to disagree," I say dejectedly. "Let's get this over with."

Each of the handsome kings kisses me on the way out and AJ begins her work. It takes all of five minutes before Rain is fussing and we have to take a break for me to get her set up in a swing.

Two hours later--two very long two hours later--AJ and her minions have determined I am ready.

They pull over the full-length mirror and I gasp as I study myself.

My sleeveless A-line gown is made of layers of cream silk chiffon with flowers embroidered along the hem... just like Rain's. My dark hair is woven into braids with tiny gemstones dotting them, and my makeup is dramatic and expertly applied.

I smile. "Let's do this."

I turn to leave, but AJ stops me and pulls out a tray with two shot glasses from Morgan's filled with Powers Irish Whiskey. This was always her go-to when she was stealing liquor, and now the name has made it my preferred pour as well.

She raises one. "May the best of our past, be the

worst of our future." She reflexively places a hand over the pendant resting at her heart as she speaks.

We clink glasses and drink, then hug. I pick up Rain, who instantly wants to catch all the gemstones in my hair, and we walk to our future.

This castle was repaired from the remains of the school the Sexies all attended in their youth. It was abandoned during the war, as was the original kingdom of the witches. In the last few months, this and the other lands have been undergoing repairs, with all races working together to lend their skills to the tasks.

It hasn't always been easy, and there has been some in-fighting--but we are turning a corner. Today will mark a new path for all our people.

The guys are waiting for us when we arrive in a large sitting room at the opposite end of the castle. They are all dressed in the formal royal style of their kingdoms, and all three are wearing their crowns.

I can hear music coming from the courtyard out front, and people cheering.

My palms are suddenly sweaty, and Rune takes my hand, letting his calm slip through me.

I smile appreciatively and straighten my back while handing my child to AJ.

French doors lead out to a balcony. Sheer curtains

hang in front of the glass so I can't quite see the crowd gathered below. Just a couple more seconds of pretending this isn't a big deal before it becomes obvious it's the biggest deal ever.

A vampire and a werewolf stand at each side of the French doors, and they pull them open when AJ gives them the go ahead. The kings walk out first, taking their seats on the lower level of the two-tiered balcony. I walk out behind them, AJ at my side, the Last Witch cradled in her arms.

Except she's not going to be the Last Witch. We made sure of that. And that's why this massive court-yard is flooded with people from all the races who have come to bear witness to this momentous occasion.

I step toward a large, elegant throne, made from the elder woods of Aevelairith, brandished in the fires of Vaemore, and carved with bones of the felled warriors in Wiceraweil. My three kings watch me take my seat, looks of absolute pride and adoration on all of their faces. When I sit, the Sexies take their own thrones. When the crowd sees us all seated, the vision of unity sends them into a frenzy of applause.

As the noise finally subsides, Rune rises and speaks.

"Today we unite our kingdoms in a way never

before seen in our world," the fae says, capturing the attention of the audience easily with his eloquence and charisma. "As kings of our respective kingdoms, we each here today lay our crowns at the feet of the True Queen, Bernadette Morgan, who returned magic to our lands, who brought us together after centuries of war, and who now leads us forward to a bright, peaceful future."

Cries of joy fill the air and my cheeks burn that all of this is for me.

But not me. Not really. None of this could have been done by one person alone. I had a lot of help from those who are here with me, and just as much from some who have gone.

Zev covers my shoulders in the royal mantle of his people, a deep purple fur-trimmed cloak.

Darius hands me the golden scepter from his kingdom, with an obsidian crystal at its head.

And Rune places the crown on my head--a special piece crafted by the Dryad queen, using bark from the Tree of Life and the scale of my dear dragon. It's a living crown, to symbolize the life I am bringing back to this world.

The gravity of the moment feels almost overwhelming as Rune gently sets the crown atop my head. The touch sends shivers through me, as the piece is practically weightless and yet carries the weight of the world all at once.

When the cheering dies down, I hold up my scepter to address the crowd.

"While I may hold this seat, it is not my accomplishments alone that brought us to this day. No amount of magic can match the power created by you, all of you, finding unity when it mattered most. By forming alliances even when you had cause to fear, resent, or hate. By trusting me to bring about a new vision for this world."

I take a moment to look at my trio of kings. Once friends, then enemies, and now truly family. I glance back at AJ, who has always been more family than friend. My eyes finally fall on Rain, who isn't friend or family. She is my heart.

I can't stop the tears from running down my cheeks as I give the final part of my speech.

"Our kingdoms are not bound by treaty or pledge. No one swears an oath or follows the words of an ancient prophecy. We share something much greater. Much truer. It is love that has brought us together, and love that welcomed magic back into the land. As long as that is true, we cannot fail." I choke up a little on my last line, but it doesn't matter because the people have already lost it. They scream and cheer and hug and smile. All they've ever known is war and hate, and this move toward peace and the common good has everyone beside themselves with joy.

I look down at my men, and they are absolutely beaming.

When I look at my daughter in AJ's arms, I see her smiling. Then she laughs and holds up two glowing silver hands. She claps and fireworks spark all around us.

It startles the shit out of me. For a second I worry the way any mother would if fire came out of their kid. Then I remember who--and what--my kid is.

This is just the beginning of what my magical ball of love will be able to do.

What a crazy baby book she's going to have.

ABOUT KARPOV KINRADE

Karpov Kinrade is the pen name for the husband and wife writing duo of USA TODAY bestselling, award-winning authors Lux Karpov-Kinrade and Dmytry Karpov-Kinrade.

Together, they live in Ukiah, California and write fantasy and science fiction novels and screenplays, make music and direct movies.

Look for more from Karpov Kinrade in *The Night Firm, Vampire Girl, The Last Witch, Dungeon Queen, The Witch's Heart, Of Dreams and Dragons, Nightfall Academy* and *Paranormal Spy Academy*. If you're looking for their suspense and romance titles, you'll now find those under Alex Lux.

They live with their three teens who share a genius for all things creative, and seven cats who think they rule the world (spoiler, they do.)

Want their books and music before anyone else and also enjoy weekly interactive flash fiction? Join them on Patreon at Patreon.com/karpovkinrade

Find them online at KarpovKinrade.com

On Facebook /KarpovKinrade

On Twitter @KarpovKinrade

And subscribe to their newsletter at ReadKK.com for special deals and up-to-date notice of new launches.

~ ~ ~ ~ ~

If you enjoyed this book, consider supporting the author by leaving a review wherever you purchased this book. Thank you.

ABOUT EVAN GAUSTAD

Evan grew up in Northern California before moving to Los Angeles in 2001. He worked as an actor and a writer in LA until 2015, and now splits his time between writing and running the drama department at the School of Performing Arts and Cultural Education in Ukiah, CA.

Follow him on Amazon.

A series about that time the world didn't end even though it was supposed to.

by Evan Gaustad and Clint Gage

It's Not the End of the World (Sisyphus Series, Book 1)

Countdown Phoenix (Sisyphus Series, Book 2)

A reverse harem paranormal romance with humor and good liquor. (with Karpov Kinrade)

The Last Witch

A Werewolf, A Vampire, and A Fae Walk Into A Bar (The Last Witch, 1)

A Werewolf, A Vampire, and A Fae Go To Budapest (The Last Witch, 2)

A Werewolf, A Vampire, and a Fae Go Home (The Last Witch, 3)

Made in United States
North Haven, CT
29 January 2023

31826022R00183